(c) 2020 Patricia M. Bryce

All rights reserved. No part of this book may be reproduced without the permission

of the publisher.

Cover Design by PaisleyRose Designs

This is a work of fiction. Names, characters, places, events, and incidents are either the products of the author's imagination or used in a fictitious manner. Any resemblance to actual persons, living or dead, or actual events is purely coincidental.

Dedicated to Charlotte-Marie
And to
Auntie Cousin Barbara McGovern
Who was a Shieldmaiden, in her own right

SIGN OF THE RAVEN

Chapter 1.

Barbara Gowan had spent so much of her life out of step with her classmates, she accepted it as normal. While others had nice homes, and siblings, she had nothing to call her own, save for the drab school uniform she wore. Even that wasn't really her's, it had been purchased by the Sisters with funds wrestled from her string on Guardians. Having been passed from one relation to another since the death of her parents when she was only five, there was little else that she could do but accept what fate had handed her. Her life was a mystery.

One memory haunted her, of how in the dead of night with only one little pitiful suitcase, she'd been delivered to the offices of Mother Superior at St. Mary's School for Girls. The Sisters of Good Hope didn't quite know what to do with her, since she wasn't old enough for regular classes. Mother Superior was at a loss, tuitions, initial uniform fees, and boarding were all paid well in advance, as well as a generous donation. However, with the fees and donation came stipulations. It was a very great sum of money, one that even the most religious Sister wasn't about to turn a nose up at. All just to keep one child.

Perhaps had the school not been in such financial need, Mother Angelica would have turned down the request. However, with the school in danger of having to be closed, even with full attendance, and the loss of support from the dioceses, Mother Superior chose to look at the situation as a gift from God. One didn't just turn up their nose at a gift from God. They accepted the child, and the stipulations to her enrollment.

The instructions from Mrs. Gowan, the child's Grandmother and guardian were strident, she considered the child a *demon spawn* and had no wish to have contact with her at all. The child was to be kept at the convent school year-round, she was to be educated with only the basics, and no frills. There would be no music, no art or any other lessons that were considered frivolous by Mrs. Gowan. The child was to be taught to be useful, and never pampered. The money, the letter

3

and the child had all been dropped on Mother Angelica at the worst of times. Mrs. Gowan's *generous patronage* donation as well as her full payment up front of tuition had caused the Nun in charge to put aside her misgivings and any questions one would ask. This patronage would save the school and convent for years to come. What did it matter if the patron's demands were unconventional?

"Do you know where you are, Barbara?" Mother Angelica asked.

"No, ma`am." She answered back in a quivering voice. The nun towered over her, all black and white and stiff. Barbara was frightened, as any young child would be. No one had told her anything, not where her mother and father were, not why she was being dragged from her bed, not where she was going.

Beside the woman questioning her stood another Sister, whose face would later become etched in Barbara's mind forever. Sister Mary Joseph, her hands slipped into her sleeves, and her face filled with dark fury. "It doesn't matter if she knows where she is, she's here, and it is our duty to direct her life," this other insisted gravely.

"This is Saint Mary's School," the tall dark woman said in a voice that reverberated. "This will be your home for now." She took firm hold of Barbara's hand and led her to the dormitory. "We will find you a bed for tonight."

"Mother, I must protest," Sister Mary Joseph complained. "You cannot put this creature in with the other girls."

"And where would you have me put her?" Mother questioned harshly. "In one of our cells?"

"What is wrong with that?" Sister Mary Joseph retorted, "A life of prayer and repentance is what her Grandmother requested for this creature."

Mother Angelica took exception being talked to in a manner that she felt was disrespectful from one of the Sisters. "I sense your hand in this child being here," she accused. "I cannot prove it, but I warn you now, Sister, I will not tolerate this child being mistreated by anyone.

SIGN OF THE RAVEN

Not even in the name of God." She looked at the frightened little girl whose hand she held. "There is a room off the dorms, she can sleep there." She led the child to the room. "This is where you will sleep, Barbara."

"My name is Barra," she said softly.

"Insolent child," Sister Mary Joseph muttered, "Your name is Barbara."

She pulled back, fearful of the woman who was angry. Mother Angelica said, "You are Barbara Gowan," she corrected softly, "We don't go by nicknames here, only proper names." She motioned the other Sister to stay outside the room, "I'll show you your room."

The room was little better than a cell, it held a bed, a dresser, and a chair. There was a small closet, which over the years held the two uniforms she granted per year. The only decoration on the dull gray wall was a crucifix. The bed was small and had only one blanket, no pillow. Here Barbara, as she now began to think of herself, spent her first terrifying night alone. In her mind she could still see the men who had ripped her from the warmth of her bed. Men who had held guns drawn on poor Mrs. Torrington as she protested their being in the house. It was a night of bad dreams and fears.

She didn't fit in; she was far younger than the rest of the student body. To make matters worse, she cried every night of the first week being at the school, disturbing the sleep of the other girls in the dorm. Even the youngest girl in the dorm was cruel to her in retaliation. When she asked where her parents were, Sister Mary Joseph slapped her for being impertinent. The strike was so brutal, Barbara lost consciousness. After waking up in the school infirmary, Barbara didn't ask any other questions. Fearful of being struck again. For the first month, the sight of that one nun would cause the child to flinch. Her reaction to Sister Mary Joseph didn't go unnoticed.

Mother Angelica watched them both like a hawk. She warned the Sister to tread lightly, and not to terrorize the child. Her warnings went unheeded. Sister Mary Joseph was stalking the little girl and took great joy in punishing her. For fear of what this woman was capable of, Mother Angelica demanded that she be reassigned. Even after Sister Mary Joseph had been reassigned, Barbara feared being struck and learned to not ask questions or to challenge the Sister's authority.

Shortly after she turned six, she was brought to a room where a doctor examined her arm. It appeared that a birthmark was being examined, and someone in the other room was demanding it be removed as it was clearly the sign of the devil. Barbara heard a woman order the doctor to remove the arm if need be. Even when she heard the doctor refuse, she feared that the woman who she didn't see would do something to make sure the arm was removed. For months she barely slept for fear of someone taking her arm.

By the time she was twelve she'd gone through two more guardians', sight unseen, was on guardian number four, and placed in another convent boarding school that went through the high school grades. There she stayed until she turned seventeen when she was awarded the scholarship that changed her residence, and her life.

Everything in her life was a dull gray mystery, right down to the strange mark on her right arm. Her life with her parents had turned into a shrouded mystery, a veiled memory. As there were no family pictures for her to keep, the images of her parents in her mind's eye began to grow gray and faded in her mind. The only last name she had ever heard after that fateful day she was delivered to the convent was that of Gowan, it turned into the only name she knew. All her mother's relations hated her for some reason, none of them would even speak to her let alone see her. There were never cards for birthdays, or letters. She was isolated. Not one of the succession of guardians after her Grandmother had bothered to come and visit her. She never left the convent, not even for holidays or vacations. She wasn't allowed to play on the playground with the other girls. She wasn't allowed to go to movies or watch television in the common room, she wasn't allowed to go on field trips. She wasn't even allowed to sit with the other students during meals or mass. She was isolated and told to pray for her own soul.

When she arrived at the college campus, it was just one more dorm room in a secession of dorm rooms as far as she was concerned. The difference here, was there were no nuns to stand over her, glaring at her as if she were the *Devil's spawn*. Her roommate was hardly ever in the room, leaving Barbara with time to make herself at home. The first week of classes she mostly listened, but the second week she began to feel free to ask questions and make inquires. At first, she had hesitated, fearing repercussions as there had been in elementary and middle school. Seeing that no one talked her down, or reprimanded her, she slowly eased into the freedom of asking for more information, or countering what had been said. By the third week of classes, she was establishing her own status and academic character.

It was shortly thereafter she was having lunch alone in the cafeteria when she was approached by two other students, a rather unlikely looking couple. Because they didn't look like the rah-rah types who were the majority of the campus, she looked up when they took seats at her table. She was about to protest their taking seats when the girl spoke.

"You're Barbara Gowan, aren't you," the girl asked in a hesitant voice. "I'm Caitlyn O'Hare and this is Tim Boyle."

Barbara looked at them, "Hello," she said cautiously. She'd never been approached by anyone before. Not in grade school, and certainly not in high school; not for any reason. She wasn't sure what to expect from this pair. He looked like he was dressed like someone ready to go to work in some field or under a truck, and she was dressed like she was about to go to tea. They didn't look like they should be together, yet clearly, they were a couple.

"You're in my Early European history class," the girl said, almost giddily. Barbara was on the verge of saying something when the other girl went on excitedly, "I thought your answers in class yesterday were so insightful. In fact, it was brilliant, even the instructor was amazed that someone got it."

"Thank you," accepting a complement wasn't easy, and Barbara wished they would go away. She wasn't used to conversation, nor to keeping company. The pair opposite her made her feel a little nervous.

"We were wondering if you'd like to form a study group." Tim said boldly, not going along with the complementary tact his girlfriend was taking. He was direct, straightforward and Barbara had a feeling he was brutally honest after his next statement. "We need a brainy person to get us through the guff. And you've got more brains than the rest of us."

"Tim," Caitlyn moaned. "That's not how to do this." Barbara decided this was the negotiator. "You'll have to excuse Tim, he's blunt."

Barbara stared for a moment, then burst out laughing. It was the first time she'd done so in a long time without fear of being reprimanded. "I'd love to," she said when she caught her breath. "But where would we do this? I can't ask you up to my dorm room, it's a broom-closet with beds." She also didn't want to run afoul of her roomie, whom she didn't really know.

"The Student Union coffee house has meeting rooms," Tim said, sounding as if he'd had expected her to know this. "I'll make arrangements with them. What night is good for you?"

"My schedule is open," Barbara assured them. "You pick the day and time, I'll be there."

"This is going to be so great!" Caitlyn said, beating her fists gently against the tabletop. Barbara wished she'd felt the freedom to do so as well, the other girls enthusiasm was contagious. "With your help, we'll all be able to pass the history course."

The time and day were set, and Barbara found she was looking forward to being part of a group for the first time. Even if it was only a study group, it was a start. For the first time, she would be part of something more than just herself. On the evening of the first meeting, she walked over to the Student Union early. She wanted to get a feel for the place. She was surprised to meet Caitlyn on the way over.

"Where's Tim?" Barbara inquired. "He didn't have second thoughts, did he?"

"Oh, he'll meet us there, he had a late class," Caitlyn said lightly. "He's really glad that you agreed to join us, he's all over the map with the class and can't seem to focus."

"It's not that hard," Barbara argued. "It's a basic history class."

"Tim needs someone to map it out for him, he won't listen to me." Caitlyn explained. "Some of the others just need to understand why this is an important class."

Barbara nodded, as if she understood, "Have you known him a long time?" she asked.

"All my life," Caitlyn answered without hesitation. "We went to grade school and high school together. You're not from around here, are you?"

"No," Barbara admitted without giving details. "Are you having any trouble with the material?"

Caitlyn smiled slyly, "No, but I'm a nerd." She shrugged, "I love the time period we are studying, and the places." She laughed, "Give me a book on the bronze age up to the iron age and I'm a happy camper!"

"Really?" Barbara mused, "I like that span also. It's unusual to find others who like it." She looked at the pretty girl standing opposite her, "If you're not having problems, why join a study group?"

"Being part of a study group on campus is a plus on ones record," Caitlyn said with positivity, "It will look great on my resume when I apply for jobs."

Barbara hadn't considered that aspect, but then she didn't think about what career she was going to seek. "I suppose it will." She agreed, not knowing what to say.

They entered the building together and Caitlyn directed Barbara to the meeting room that had been reserved for them. "They are giving us the room free, as long as we purchase our refreshments." Caitlyn warned. "They will supply whatever we order."

"That's handy," Barbara put her books down on the long table that was part of a large square of tables. "This is a nice little room," she mused.

"The Student Union is a great place for meetings," Caitlyn agreed. "A lot of groups meet here."

"Are there other study groups?"

"Sure," Caitlyn said, "not everyone is as brainy as you are."

"I'm not that brainy," Barbara said. "I just haven't had many distractions."

"I've had plenty," Caitlyn laughed, "I'm one of eight children, dead center, in the pack."

"I'm an only child," Barbara said before she thought about it.

"Oh," Caitlyn's reaction was mild, but Barbara hadn't given her much to go on. "Your folks must be very proud of you." She said politely.

"I'm an orphan." Barbara took a seat, not realizing how her statement had affected the other. "I've a guardian, that I never see."

Caitlyn sat down beside her, "OH no," she said with real sadness. "That's awful."

"It's okay, it's all I've ever known, so I don't mind." She assured the other. "How many others are we expecting?" she looked at the other seats and the number of water glasses on the table.

"At least a dozen others," Caitlyn said. "You'll like them. Some are in class with you and I, others just need the extra boost of a focused group. Most are from around here, and you'll like them."

Caitlyn had been right; Barbara did like the others. They were all interested in the course they were taking, even if they didn't understand some of what was written in the book. Tim asked good questions, and Ray Housemen brought up interesting conflicts. They were a lively bunch, and Barbara had a great time being with them. For the first time in her life, she enjoyed other students. She looked forward to the next group meeting the next week.

When the second meeting was over Tim invited Barbara to accompany him and Caitlyn to the farmer's market on the upcoming Saturday. "It'll be a fantastic time," he explained. "They always have the neatest crafts in the fall."

"How do you know about this?" Barbara asked.

"I grew up here," Tim said. "My older brother attended this college; my folks live just three miles away."

"That's so nice," Barbara said. "You've got history."

"Everyone has a history," Caitlyn said, hooking arms with Barbara as they exited the Union building. "Tim's and mine is connected to this town, and this school and the farmer's market."

"I don't have that." Barbara said quietly.

Tim stopped, "What do you mean, you don't have that?" He was troubled. "Where did you go to grade school?" He challenged.

"St. Mary of the Dragon; followed by Our Lady of Lost hope." Barbara murmured. It was how she had thought of those places, and it came out before she could stop herself. In her mind she'd even dubbed the sisters, The Sisters of No Hope.

"Where?" Tim gasped.

"Sorry," she said waving a hand, "St. Mary's convent school for girls in Stanhope, what I said before is how the girls attending the convent school thought of the place. An in joke if you will." Barbara didn't like talking about those places. She hated thinking about them, about the nuns, about the loneliness. It brought back too many bad memories and the nightmares of her first night.

"Who sent you *there*?" he demanded, "I've read about that place, and the nuns there." He shivered visibly. "There was a state investigation into that school, they brought up some of the older nuns on charges of child abuse."

"Yeah, it was pretty miserable," Barbara admitted. "My *grandmother* sent me to St. Mary's when my parents died when I was five."

"Five? But I thought that place didn't take students under seven." Tim reached out a hand, "Why would your grandmother do such a thing?"

"I don't know, I didn't know the lady. She never bothered to visit me," Barbara answered. "I only know that my folks died, and I was sent away. When my Grandmother died, I was passed on to the next relation that became my guardian, and then to middle school and High School at Our Lady of Perpetual Hope in Cortland by the most recent guardian. I was there until I turned seventeen and got the scholarship to come here."

"How did your parents die?" Tim asked softly.

"I don't know," Barbara admitted. "There wasn't anybody to ask... the one time I did ask, a nun hit me so hard I woke up in the infirmary; I never asked again."

"Oh, you poor kid," Caitlyn sympathized. "That's child abuse. Did you report it?"

"I was five, who was I going to tell? Another nun?" Barbara said shaking her head. "I haven't told anyone about this. I don't know why I just told you."

Tim shook his head, "That's awful."

"It is what it is," Barbara said. "Please don't tell the others. I've never been treated so nice as I have been by you all and I'd hate to have them look at me with pity."

"It's our secret." Tim assured her. He placed a reassuring hand on her arm. "You'll never have to worry about pity from us."

ON SATURDAY MORNING, they showed up at Barbara's dorm room early. Luckily, her roommate was nowhere to be found. "They

SIGN OF THE RAVEN

have coffee and fresh made apple cider doughnuts, and mulled cider!" Tim announced when they came into her room. "But you have to get there early to get the best table and the freshest doughnuts." He looked about the room, "You described it right, broom closet with beds." He joked.

"This is roomier than the room I had at the Convent school, if you can imagine that," Barbara said, slipping into a dark sweater. "Will this market even be open?"

"We always get there as they are setting up," Caitlyn agreed with Tim's assessment. "And today is just glorious outside! The sun is shining, and the air is crisp! It's a great day for a nice walk."

"Shake a leg, Barbara," Tim commanded. "This man needs his coffee!" He made a rolling motion with his hand to hurry her.

Caitlyn looked at the empty made up bed across the room, "Your roomie up and out early?"

"Never came in last night," Barbara countered. "I have seen her a handful of times since moving in. She's never here, and when she is, we don't talk. I don't even know her name."

"Her loss," Tim said as he opened the door, "Come on, I need coffee and doughnuts! Have you ever had fresh cider doughnuts?"

The Farmer's Market was set up in the large parking lot of the Pilgrim Methodist Church. There were produce stalls, and craft tables, and a line to get in. Even early, there was a line and people were friendly, greeting each other and calling out to get a table at the coffee, doughnut stand. Tim got in line, and the girls grabbed a table on the outer fringes of the area. There were college students, locals, and out of towners at this market. It seemed that the coffee area was one of the most popular places. Barbara had to admit that Tim was right, the coffee was amazing, and the doughnuts were to die for. So much so, that Barbara indulged in three before she realized it. She'd have loved a fourth but could hear Sister Mary Joseph's voice in her head calling her a glutton.

When they finished their coffee and doughnuts, Tim bought each of them a mug of cider to go.

They spent the day perusing the different stalls and looking for craft bargains for Caitlyn. She said she was doing a bit of early holiday shopping. Barbara wished she had someone to buy for, let alone extra cash to pay for purchases. They bought apples and the last of the seasons' peaches and ate lunch in a little makeshift café. When they were done, Tim and Caitlyn walked Barbara back toward the dorms on campus.

"Thanks for the outing," Barbara said. "I had fun."

"Put it on your calendar for next week too," Tim said, an arm hung on Caitlyn's shoulders. "We'll make it our Saturday morning routine, until they close up for the season."

"You sure I'm not a fifth wheel?" Barbara asked feeling a bit like a fish out of water. "I mean you two are sort of a couple, aren't you?"

"Yeah," Tim said, "We are, but you're our friend."

"I haven't seen you exactly socializing with anyone else," Caitlyn observed. "Tim and I get lots of alone time, spending a morning with you is fun for us. Plus you get a guided tour of the campus and the town."

"I'm still not used to being out in the real world," Barbara admitted. "Actually, I feel like a foreigner. I'm regimented to convent life."

Tim shook his head, "That sucks." He shrugged, "So think of us as your guides into the world. Or at least into the world of Stonewall Campus and the town of Danbury."

"Okay," she agreed. "I am glad to have the help."

"We'll see you in class on Monday," Caitlyn said taking Tim's hand. "And then study group Tuesday night; we should order pizza!"

"Sounds good," Barbara nodded. She'd heard of pizza, but it wasn't something the Convent served. She looked forward to trying it for the first time.

SIGN OF THE RAVEN

THE NEXT FEW WEEKS flew by, they attended the last Farmer's market on the last Saturday of October and then switched to having coffee at a little café in town on Saturday mornings.

"Do you have plans for Thanksgiving?" Caitlyn asked. She placed her coffee down and smiled at Barbara.

"Just a lot of studying," Barbara answered shaking her head in the negative.

"You're not going... home?"

Barbara hated the upset look on Caitlyn's face. "No, there isn't a home for me to go to," she said resolutely. She wasn't about to tell her friend that she hadn't been invited to her guardian's home for the holiday. It sounded pitiful, and Barbara hated pity. "But it's okay, I usually stay on campus for these occasions." She flinched, that sounded worse. She didn't want her new friend thinking of her as an orphan out of some novel. "I get a lot of extra studying done. How did you think I got to be so brainy?"

Caitlyn shook her head, "You're coming to my house."

"Don't your folks have enough people to feed?" Barbara teased. "You said you're one of eight siblings."

"They won't notice one more," Caitlyn said. "I'll pick you up after classes on Wednesday and you can spend the entire weekend with me."

"That's too kind," Barbara protested, "Won't you want to spend time with Tim here?"

"I'll be glued to the tv football games with my dad and grand dad, and older brother," Tim warned. "It's a Boyle tradition, and I'm not messing with it." He pointed to his girlfriend, "She hates football."

"See?" Caitlyn gave her a soulful look, "I need you, girlfriend, so say you'll come."

"But your house is full, you said you're one of eight kids!" Barbara argued. She wasn't sure if she was trying to spare Caitlyn and her family the burden of a guest, or herself the burden of being a guest.

"And what's one more?" Caitlyn countered. "My one sister and brother will only be there with their spouses and kids on the day of thanksgiving. Nana and PawPaw will arrive early on Wednesday, and so will my aunt and uncle. It's a big old farmhouse, there's lots of room."

"I don't want to impose," Barbara was fighting a losing battle.

"I have a big room all to myself," Caitlyn argued. "I haven't had a good old-fashioned sleep over since I was sixteen, it'll be fun." She promised.

"What's a sleep over?" Barbara inquired.

Caitlyn looked at her, "You're kidding," Caitlyn giggled, then stopped. "No, you're not. You've never had a sleep over?" Caitlyn looked horrified.

"You're not going to let this go, are you?" Barbara watched as the other girl shook her head and all that curly red hair shook. "Fine, if it's okay with your folks, I'll be happy to spend the holiday with you." She didn't want to see pity on her friend's face, she didn't want to tell her all that she'd missed growing up in the convent.

Wednesday morning, after her shower, Barbara found a note from her roomie telling her she had the room for the weekend. She packed a bag, and left it on her bed, figuring that Caitlyn would let her pick it up on their way off campus. She was surprised at how few students made it to class, but the instructors didn't seem to be bothered. It was after all a half day, and the fewer students, the easier the day.

THE O'HARE HOUSE WAS more than just a big old farmhouse. It was also loud, full of chaos and love. Mrs. O'Hare, Caitlyn's mom was up to her elbows in pie dough when the girls arrived. Never having met any parents of her classmates before, Barbara wasn't sure what to expect. Mrs. O'Hare was very much like an older version of Caitlyn. She was tall and fair skinned, with an abundance of red hair wound up in a knot on the top of her head. Her blue eyes were full of merriment and laughter, and her voice was pleasant and even.

"Caiti," she said, breathlessly, "at last! Your sister Molly has choir and I have to get these pies done, mind lending a hand?"

"Happy to," Caitlyn said. "Mom, this is Barbara."

"Welcome to Bedlam," Mrs. O'Hare greeted her with a wave at her kitchen. "I hope you don't regret your stay."

"Could I lend a hand, too?" Barbara asked.

"The more the merrier." Mrs. O'Hare called as she returned to rolling out dough. "Caiti will show you where we keep the aprons. I'm not about to turn down help."

"You sure you want to?" Caitlyn whispered.

"It was the one thing I liked at the convent school I attended, helping in the kitchen." Barbara whispered back. She tied on the old-fashioned yoked apron and began to assemble pies with skills she'd developed over many years.

"Someone knows their way around a kitchen," Mrs. O'Hare complemented.

"Yes, ma'am," Barbara agreed. "Apple, mince and pumpkin? Seems like a lot of pies."

"And they'll be all gone before you know it," Mrs. O'Hare complained. "Oh, dear, I've made too much dough again."

"We could do some cinnamon wreaths," Barbara suggested. Caitlyn's mom motioned to Barbara to go ahead.

"Did Nana and PawPaw get in alright?" Caitlyn asked as she worked on mixing the pumpkin pie filling.

"Yes, they are resting in their room," her mother answered. "Your Aunt Mary and Uncle Don will be here in an hour. And your sister, Joyce isn't coming at all this year. Little Petey is down with chickenpox."

"I have two married sisters, one married brother, one brother who is in the marines. Then comes me, my brother James who is a senior in high school, my sister Molly who is a freshman in high school and my youngest brother, Davy who is in eighth grade." Caitlyn explained.

"Lovely," Barbara said.

"Caiti tells me you're an only child." Mrs. O'Hare said.

"Yes," Barbara kept working on her cinnamon wreaths. "This is a lovely change for me, being surrounded by a large family."

"I'm glad you think so," Caitlyn's mom said happily. "Would one of you girls pull the bread out of the oven?" The buzzer was going off and she was still working on the apple lattice.

"I'll get it," Barbara offered.

"We'll be having stew tonight," Mrs. O'Hare said. "I love crockpots! I've had two of them going since morning."

"I love your kitchen," Barbara complemented, "It's so big and friendly and organized."

"With this crew one has to be," a man said coming into the kitchen from outdoors. "Honey, I'm home," he moved to Mrs. O'Hare and kissed her. He was taller than his wife and dressed in a business suit. His hair was a shared darker auburn than his wife's red. His eyes were gray. His open affection for his wife made Barbara wonder about her own parents.

"Dad, this is Barbara, Barbara, my dad," Caitlyn said.

"Hello, Barbara," he said with a smile, "so you're the girl who has our Caiti all excited again about history."

"I don't know about that," Barbara felt her cheeks flush with color. "I only know that it's a lively study group, and Caitlyn has a lot of input."

"That's good to hear," Caitlyn's dad said. He looked about the kitchen, "Smells great in here, ladies."

"Thanks Daddy!" Caitlyn said. "Wait until you see what Barbara did with the extra pie dough!"

SIGN OF THE RAVEN

He looked at the wreaths coming out of one of the ovens, "Looks wonderful." He smiled. "I'll clear out, so you can finish up, I'll go check on your folks." He told his wife.

"Dinner will be ready in an hour," she promised.

"Nana, and PawPaw are your mom's parents," Barbara commented, making mental notes.

"Yeah, Dad's folks live in Arizona, they moved there when I was ten. Gramps O'Hare has a condition that needed dryer air." Caitlyn explained. "They only come in for weddings, graduations and that sort of thing. We go out there in the spring for one week at Easter."

"I'm sure you must have similar arrangements," Mrs. O'Hare said breezily.

"Not really," Barbara said quietly. "I've got a guardian that I've never formally met." She hadn't even thought about the fact that it was unusual, or that Caitlyn's mother would react. She answered before she thought it out. Something about being in this house made her feel free to be honest.

Mrs. O'Hare halted what she was about to do, turned to look at Barbara. "I beg your pardon?"

"I'm an orphan," Barbara said without emotion. "So, this," she waved at the kitchen and the activity, "is all new to me." Seeing the stark look of sadness and frustration on Caitlyn's mom's face, Barbara added. "It's okay... I've been an orphan since I was five, I'm used to it."

"You poor dear," Mrs. O'Hare sympathized, she had forgotten what she was doing and took a seat. "What do you mean, you've never met *this* guardian?"

"This is the latest guardian," Barbara explained, again without emotions. "My mother's mother was the first when I was five. I've had three or four, I've lost count. None of them ever wanted to meet me."

Mrs. O'Hare looked at Caitlyn, "You knew this?"

"Most of it," Caitlyn nodded. "I just couldn't bear the thought of Barbara all alone and eating God knows what. The cafeteria is closed on Holidays, and she doesn't really know Danbury very well."

Barbara took the pie that was now sitting on the counter in front of Mrs. O'Hare, "Let me get that in the oven for you."

"Oh my, what am I doing?" Mrs. O'Hare whispered.

"Feeling sorry for me," Barbara suggested. "But don't, I'm fine. You can't miss what you never had."

"You're too young to be so cynical," Mrs. O'Hare warned. "Where did you spend your holidays?"

"Until recently, I've lived in Convent schools. I've spent my holidays and my summers with the nuns." Barbara said. "Most of the sisters were pretty decent, and thoughtful." Barbara had a sudden wish that she'd not told Caitlyn about the slap incident. "I learned early on to not ask too many questions, and to do as I was told." She explained. "I did enjoy holidays because they let me work in the kitchen."

"Surely your grandmother visited," Mrs. O'Hare said.

"No," Barbara shook her head. "I don't know what kind of relationship my mother had with my grandmother, but while she was my guardian, she never wanted to see me."

Mrs. O'Hare stared, "That's Machiavellian."

Barbara took a seat across from the woman seated at the center island in the kitchen, "I hesitated to tell Caitlyn my circumstances," she admitted. "It doesn't sound real, does it?"

"It sounds like something from Charles Dickens." Mrs. O'Hare murmured. She reached a handout to Barbara, "We'll try to make this a good Thanksgiving for you."

"It already is," Barbara assured her.

LATER, UPSTAIRS IN Caitlyn's room, Barbara thanked her friend again for the invitation. "I can't thank you enough for asking me to spend this weekend with your family. Your parents are wonderful, and I love your family."

"They are fun, aren't they?" Caitlyn responded, "What were your parents like?"

"I don't remember," Barbara replied quietly. "Right now, they are sort of faded figures."

"Don't you have photos?" Caitlyn asked.

"No," Barbara drew her legs up until her chin rested on her knees on the bed she was sitting on. "I don't have anything from my life with them. It's like someone tried to wipe them from existence, and only I remain. I sometimes feel that if she could have, my grandmother would have wiped me from existence as well."

Caitlyn took a seat on the same bed, and held out a hand, "That's awful."

Barbara took a deep long breath, letting it out slowly. "While I was living at the convent school, I didn't ask too many questions. And because I'm still legally underage, and under the control of my guardian, I'm still not asking too many." She confessed, "But I intend to ask a lot of questions once I turn 21. I want answers."

"You have to wait that long?"

"Financially, I'm still under the jurisdiction and management of my guardian." Barbara explained. "While my scholarship covers my books and my boarding, I'm legally under her control." Another deep sigh escaped her lips. "She wasn't happy that I got this scholarship, she wanted me to enter the convent after I graduated high school and take vows."

"You're kidding," Caitlyn gasped.

"No, I'm not." Barbara said. "I wish I was, but I'm not."

"But that's... nuts..." Caitlyn complained. "In this day and age? How could anyone make such a demand?"

"This whole thing is nuts, if you ask me," Barbara agreed. "My life up until I arrived here has been dictated to and arranged. I feel like a fish out of water most of the time here. I'm socially awkward, and backward when it comes to the simplest of things."

"No, you're not," Caitlyn said, supportively. "You're great with our study group."

"Caitlyn," Barbara whispered, "I don't even know how to use makeup. It wasn't allowed at the convent school." Her friend stared at her. "That third meeting of our study group was the first time I ever ate pizza!"

"I had no idea." Her friend's face blanched at the memory, "I thought you were just enjoying it."

"I'm working at not drawing attention," Barbara explained. "But I'm worried that someone is going to catch on, really fast." She fought the tears that were stinging and threatening to come. "I mean, how long will it take before they realize I always wear the same thing?"

"What do you mean?"

"My guardian didn't want me coming here at all, she had to be strong armed by the new Bishop into allowing me to accept the scholarship." Barbara said. "He informed her that I'd get a better education with the scholarship than they could give me. Her answer was I didn't need better, that she wanted me to become a nun."

"That's terrible." Caitlyn answered. "What did the Bishop say to her?"

"He told her that wasn't her choice to make, that he didn't think I was being called to be a nun. He told her that it was the scholarship, or I'd be shipped to her. So, scholarship won, but she refused the nun's request to supply me a proper wardrobe. The scholarship covers my books and supplies, my room and board, but not clothes." Barbara whispered. "What you see, came out of the church's mission box. I have three changes of clothes and that's it, and it's all pretty somber. I was lucky the poor didn't want these." She motioned to her attire.

"Oh, Barbara, you must forgive me," Caitlyn covered her eyes for a moment, then looked at Barbara, "I thought you were a Goth."

SIGN OF THE RAVEN

"Goth?" Barbara murmured, "I don't even know what that means."

"It's a style," Caitlyn assured her, "a fashion statement. Mostly blacks and grays."

"Caitlyn," Barbara gulped and shook her head, "I know it's asking a lot, but I was hoping that you could... help me." She went on. "All the time I spent at the convent; my guardians were required to make sure I had an allowance. They were not happy about it, but it was arranged. However, because I never went out, I never had anything to spend it on," she explained. "The nuns never took me shopping, expect when they needed help with carrying groceries, or I needed a new uniform." She went on. "I have money, but no familiarity with buying clothes or makeup... could you help me...?"

"How much money do you have?" Caitlyn asked.

"Enough for essentials." Barbara said. "I would just like to look like I don't stand out so much."

Caitlyn shrugged, "I'll be happy to help, but I kinda think the goth look suits you. Please don't be offended. Maybe if we added makeup...." Again, she shrugged. "What do you consider... essential?"

"I don't even own a pair of jeans," Barbara disclosed.

Caitlyn's jaw dropped. "We'll head out early Saturday, Friday is going to be a riot out there and I refuse to part of it."

Barbara nodded; grateful her friend was willing to help.

THURSDAY WAS A BLUR when Barbara thought about it. The house was full of people, adults, kids, and loud barking dogs. Mary, the older sister who had come to the dinner, shoved her baby into Barbara's arms not even noticing she wasn't her sister Caitlyn. She was arguing with her husband who was trying to take a coat off their three-year-old who wasn't cooperating. Brother William and his wife showed up with a six-month-old offspring and joined the loud crowd. James and Davy were busy most of the morning setting up the skype to the big screen tv so that when Jason called in it would be seen by all. Caitlyn and Molly took turns filling Barbara in on who everyone was, and what was going on. Barbara's head was spinning long before dinner began.

Barbara was used to long tables, and family serving style. She listened to the conversations and joined in when invited. When Jason's face appeared on the big screen tv, the first thing he noticed was Barbara.

"Did you go and adopt someone to replace me?" he teased. Then when introduced he greeted her with instructions, "Barbara, if you're taking my place at the table, this is what you need to do, argue every point. Doesn't matter if you agree with them, take the other side."

Mr. O'Hare said, "Ignore him," and added, "he's a smart ass."

When their company that was going home left, Caitlyn and Barbara were exhausted. They retired to Caitlyn's room and crashed and burned. Friday was more of the same, and by evening, Barbara was feeling dizzy. It was after ten in the morning when they woke to the aroma of something delicious in the kitchen. Mrs. O'Hare was making waffles, while Caitlyn's dad and granddad were in the family room watching the college pregame warmups.

"Bout time you two got out of bed, everyone else has eaten. I'm making a fresh batch for you," Mrs. O'Hare teased. She poured coffee for both girls. "Nice to see you survived." She said to Barbara.

"It was amazing," Barbara said between sips, "is every holiday like this?"

"Christmas is much louder," Caitlyn said in a muffled voice between her coffee mug and her robe. "And more crowded and seems to go on forever."

Mrs. O'Hara nodded, "What plans do you two have for today?"

"Shopping at Secondhand Row," Caitlyn mumbled. "We have a list."

"For what?" her mother inquired. "You have more clothes than you know what to do with!" She scolded Caitlyn.

"A few essentials for me," Barbara said. "Jeans, sneakers, something not black."

Mrs. O'Hara laughed.

"Maybe some place to cut my hair?" Barbara suggested.

CAITLYN WAS SURPRISED when Mrs. O'Hara suggested she go with the girls, Barbara was delighted. Secondhand Row was a thrift store run by Mrs. O'Hara's friend Olivia. It had vintage, it had funk, it had BoHo, and it was reasonably priced. Several hours later, Barbara left with bags full of new or like new items including several pairs of jeans and several pair of shoes. Mrs. O'Hara made sure it was mostly essentials, and nothing frivolous. She also made sure that Barbara adhered to a budget. Because Olivia was close to Mrs. O'Hara, she gave Barbara a discount on this first shopping expedition.

The second stop had been Mrs. O'Hara's favorite hairstylist. She took one look at Barbara's long dark hair and frowned. "When was the last time you had a decent haircut?" she inquired.

"When I was five," Barbara answered. She recalled one nun taking a pair of shears to her when she was twelve. What resulted was a botched mess. Mother Angelica had been livid.

"Looks it," the woman shook her head, "Just what do you want me to do with this?"

"Fix it," Mrs. O'Hara said calmly. "At least, make her look like a normal college student."

"There are none," the stylist argued with a cigarette hanging from her lips. "But I'll do my best."

An hour later Barbara left the little salon feeling if not new, at least better than she felt before. She still looked offbeat, but at least it was a start. Her long hair was now shoulder length, and even. The stylist had given her a list of ways she could wear this style and showed her how easy upkeep would be.

"What have you been washing your face with?" The woman pulled out a magnifying glass that lit up. "My God in heaven, your pores are a mess. What kind of moisturizer are you using?"

"What's that?" Barbara asked innocently.

"Millie," Mrs. O'Hara leaned down, "she was raised in a convent."

Millie drew back, stared at Barbara for a moment, then pushed the magnifying glass out of her way. She took hold of Barbara's hands. "I'm going to teach you simple ways to take care of your hair and skin. Your skin is not peaches and cream like your friend Caitlyn here, but it's not dreadful." She assessed Barbara's features. "You've got great eyes, and we'll play them up. Nothing fancy, but a light smoky eye."

"I told you," Caitlyn bragged. "Goth."

"Not that severe," Millie countered, "softer, less dark. Trust me." She showed the novice ways to use makeup without looking over done. It was a good start. When Barbara left the shop, it was with a new outlook and a new style.

Chapter 2.

"The least you could do is come out and cheer our side on," Tim complained bitterly to Caitlyn, on Monday at lunch.

Barbara heard his pleas as she approached the table, but Caitlyn seemed totally against his suggestions. "Is this a sport event?" she asked taking her place at the table in the student union. "I didn't know you play any."

"He doesn't," Caitlyn said pointedly. "He wants me to come and watch him play a *war game* at the old, abandoned mall."

"A war game?" Barbara questioned with a cryptic smile. "Which one?"

Tim turned to look at her, "Did you cut your hair?" he asked with a bewildered stare. When she nodded with a smile, he tried to re-focus. "It's not just a war game, it's a LARP."

"What's that?" Barbara asked with a grimace.

Tim dropped his sandwich that had almost reached his open mouth and stared at her. He sputtered but couldn't seem to form words. Frustrated, he turned to Caitlyn.

"It's a role-playing game, that includes dressing up for the part," Caitlyn said bitterly. "This one thought so much of his game, he bought me a membership for my birthday."

"What's wrong with that?" Barbara asked. "Sounds thoughtful to me."

"I would have rather he bought me a good book!" Caitlyn grumbled. "I don't know why you think watching you get beaten up on a field of battle would make me happy."

"I don't get beaten up," Tim countered. "I battle in glory for the honor of our Clan!"

Caitlyn turned to Barbara and rolled her eyes, "He gets beaten to a bloody pulp, and brags about it."

"You make it sound... bad," Tim complained and looked over at Barbara before picking up his sandwich again, "It's really a lot of fun, and it's educational."

"What is this game called?" Barbara asked a bit uncertain of what she was asking.

"Conquest of Iron," Tim pulled a rule book out of his inner pocket. "This is part of the Forgotten Realms series, it's mostly fantasy, but it's supposed to be based on bronze and iron age history. It's a bit loose and fast with the history, but that's not why I like it. I like that it covers a lot of the tools and implements of that time. And you should see our weapons."

Barbara opened the book and read the first paragraph. "You weren't kidding when you said it plays fast and loose." She read the first page, "How long have you been doing this?"

"Since our junior year in High School," Caitlyn complained.

"Wait, you've been playing this, and you can't keep your facts straight in real history?" Barbara stared at him.

Tim lowered his sandwich and gulped down the mouthful in his maw, "Barb," he said, shorting her name, "If you talked about the weapons more, my mind would not wander."

"Weapons?" She challenged.

"That's what boys like," he teased. "Weapons. Sharp pointy things, and lots of em."

She looked at Caitlyn, "You've got to be kidding."

Caitlyn shook her head, "I thought he'd outgrow this, Neanderthal tendency, but no..." she crossed her arms. "No, he only got more involved."

"I'm a clan leader," Tim said proudly, "worked my way up from peasant to Clan head of family. I'm planning on becoming the Tribal leader before I'm done!"

"If he lives that long," Caitlyn retorted. "It took months last year for the bruises to fade!"

SIGN OF THE RAVEN

Barbara tried to keep a straight face, but smirked. "I see." She looked over at Caitlyn, "And you object to going and watching?"

Caitlyn made a face, "The old mall is... dirty, and rundown, and should have been condemned. I'm betting they have rats!"

"It's not that bad," Tim objected. "The building engineers say it's structurally sound."

"It stinks in there," Caitlyn complained.

"The game's board got the mall commission to clean things up and run the filtration system since you were last there. It smells fine now." Tim said between bites.

"And the rats?" Caitlyn asked.

"There were none," Tim objected, "they had the exterminators come and check." He made a face at his girlfriend. "So there, smarty."

"So, what are you?" Barbara kept reading.

"I'm a Celtic Norsemen hybrid." He answered.

Barbara looked up from the book, "You're a what?"

"Celtic Norsemen hybrid," he repeated. "And that Miss smarty-pants is historically accurate." He made another face at his girlfriend. "I checked."

Caitlyn shook her head, picked up her cellphone and opened her picture files to show Barbara a shot of Tim in costume. "I will say the boys do work on making a good show of it."

"That's very creative," Barbara nodded. "But how do you play in a mall?"

"The mall is quartered off into sections, we have spectators' areas set up for a viewing stand when we take a field. The stands are supposed to be our fortresses and lodges. We have pikes and shields decorating the areas designated to each group in the tourney. Some are trophies, but in our case it's the extra equipment." Tim explained. "Our clan is taking on the invading forces that loosely represent Anglos/Romans."

"Do you ever win?" Barbara inquired.

"Not so far," Tim sighed. "But it would be nice to have my best girl watching, even if I'm dying on the field."

Barbara tuned to Caitlyn, "This doesn't sound that bad."

"You're kidding!" Caitlyn countered.

"No, in fact," Barbara said. "I'd kind of like to attend."

Tim smiled at Caitlyn, "Come on Caiti!" he pleaded. "Barb can't sit there alone and if you two come some of the other girls will come back out."

"Agh," Caitlyn growled. "Barbara, it means dressing in a long skirt."

"I don't have one," Barbara looked at Tim. "Spectators have to dress up too?"

"Caiti has several outfits, I'm sure she could loan you one." Tim negotiated.

"You have costumes?" Barbara turned wide eyed to her friend. "OH, please, Caitlyn. I've never done anything like this. I've always wanted to get dressed up as someone else."

"Didn't the nuns ever let you go trick or treating?" her friend asked.

"No." Barbara answered. "Never." It was still a painful memory. The other girls in the boarding school had a Halloween party, but Barbara had never been invited to join in. She could hear the music and fun up in her room but had never been allowed to join.

Tim saw an opening, "Come on, Caiti! She's never even been trick or treating... this could make up for years of deprivation." Both girls turned to stare. "I'm desperate." He confessed. "I'll say and do anything right now."

Caitlyn shrugged. "Fine, I'd rather go to the art festival at Conner's Gallery, but since you both insist..." She looked at Barbara, "He's right, I do have several costumes, one is bound to fit you. He's been making me buy and make them since we were 16. Come over tomorrow after class and we'll pick one out for you."

"This is going to be fun," Barbara tuned to Tim, "mind if I keep the book to read the rules and regulations?"

"Be my guest," he said. "I've got it all memorized."

"Really?"

"No," he admitted, "just the important stuff." Both girls laughed again. He reached across the table and took Caitlyn's pickle.

THE NEXT AFTERNOON, Barbara and Caitlyn were up in her room pulling out the costumes when Mrs. O'Hara came into the room. "What's this?" she asked.

"Tim roped me into this weekend's tourney." Caitlyn admitted. "He used Barbara as bait."

Her mother sat down, covering her mouth to contain her laughter. "OH really?"

"I've never done anything like this," Barbara admitted. "And Caitlyn offered to lend me a costume."

"At least it will get some use again," Mrs. O'Hara agreed. "And they are such nice costumes; Caitlyn put a lot of effort into making them."

Caitlyn grudgingly agreed. "I'll bet her feet would fit into my old shods," she said looking down at Barbara's feet. "We never throw anything away in this house, save it for the next kid in line."

"I like that," Barbara said. "I wonder if my folks were like that."

Mrs. O'Hara looked over at her, "You don't know anything about your parents?"

"No," Barbara sat down, "and it gets kind of murky trying to tell people about it. Sounds like I'm making up a story." She looked at the costume laid out on the bed, "You made this?" she asked Caitlyn.

"Most of it," her friend nodded, "I took sewing in High School, and when Tim told me about the game, I thought it was a one-time thing, like the Halloween Party the town throws. I thought it would be fun to dress up and pretend."

"But for Tim it was more than a one-time event," Mrs. O'Hara said. "It's become an obsession."

"Every boy needs a hobby, daddy says," Caitlyn mused. "This one leaves bruises."

"They actually hit each other?" Barbara gasped.

"They aren't supposed to hit hard, but sometimes the boys on both teams get carried away." Caitlyn nodded, her red hair bouncing as she bobbed her head. "And some of the guys who play the Anglo/Romans are only too happy to smack the Celts around."

"I sense a bit of prejudice," Barbara stated.

"Maybe a touch," Mrs. O'Hara nodded in agreement. "Most of the boys in the Celtic and Norsemen group are just that, Celts and Norse. They have always taken a ribbing from the more Anglo descendants."

"And still they play with each other," Barbara mused.

"Tim really thinks that one day, the Clan will rise and win." Caitlyn complained.

"Maybe, they will." Barbara agreed.

"The green over-gown looks made for you Barbara," Mrs. O'Hara changed the subject. "I'll bet your old raw linen Viking tunic would fit her."

Caitlyn agreed, "I'll bet it would," she put a russet over gown down on her bed, "It's up in the chifforobe. I'll bet the shods are up there too. You stay here, and I'll be right back. No sense in you coming up and getting mussed up."

Mrs. O'Hara smiled, "I'm glad you got her to do this again," she confessed to Barbara, "I think sometimes Caiti forgets to do things that Tim likes, not just what she likes." She confided softly.

"They make a wonderful couple." Barbara said, not sure what else to say.

"They do," her friend's mother nodded in agreement. "But they have a way to go before they'll be ready for something more permanent. However, I want them to be equals. That means Caitlyn needs to flex a bit more when it comes to the things Tim likes. I'm glad you were interested in going, it's an encouragement that Caiti needed."

"She's a good friend," Barbara confided. "She makes me feel... normal."

Mrs. O'Hara offered her a sad, understanding, smile. "I'm glad to hear that. You've had a rough time of it, and I'm glad that Caiti is helping you find your footing here."

"I want to thank you again, for Thanksgiving." Barbara said softly. "It was wonderful."

"You're always welcome." She turned hearing Caitlyn approach.

"I've got the tunic, the shods and the underpinnings," Caitlyn announced proudly. "If we are going to do this, we are going to do this up right."

"I'm excited," Barbara giggled. "This is such fun."

"I'll let you girls get the assembles done," Caitlyn's mother said, "Come down and model for me."

Caitlyn held the raw linen tunic up to Barbara, "Mom was right, it'll fit you like a glove!"

"It's so nice," Barbara ran her fingers over the fabric, "You made this?"

"This and a few others," Caitlyn preened.

"But it's too good to lend out," Barbara protested.

"Oh no," Caitlyn argued. "I outgrew it when I was a senior, I had this growth spurt." She laughed. "My bust got much too big for it, even with a binder on."

Barbara blushed. "Oh."

"You're a bit shorter than I am, and I'll bet you'll get a couple of wears at least out of this." Caitlyn picked up the green over dress and held it up against the tunic that Barbara was wearing. "Mom's right, this is better with your coloring than mine. One would think with all this red hair, green would be my trademark color, but no."

"The russet and the golden rod are better with your coloring," Barbara agreed. "This is beautiful costuming."

"It's not totally accurate," Caitlyn confessed, "but it is fun." She held up a long-pointed finger with painted nail, "Don't you ever tell Tim I said that or I'll...." She paused. "I can't threaten you." She said. "You've had many more hard times then I can imagine." She lowered her hand, "Just don't tell, he'd never let me hear the end of it."

"I won't." Barbara promised. "What's between you and Tim isn't my business."

"It's not that I don't like dressing up, I do," Caitlyn sat down with frustrations. "It's just that, the guys on the other team," her lips thinned speaking of the opposing team, "really go out of their way to bloody up our guys."

"Is there a rivalry that I'm not aware of?" Barbara also took a seat on the bed. "I mean I thought everyone here was pretty friendly."

"It goes back to the colonial days." Caitlyn explained. "The big landowners here about were English mostly. A few sheep farmers who were Scots, they always had money and property. There were tradesmen, but they had only their store and their skills. When the revolution happened, the English landowners were still the big wheels. Most of the rest moved in and worked their way up. People like Warren Becket, and Todd Rayburn and Jason Falks, come from money. Old money. Their family roots go way back, and they don't let anyone forget it."

"And they are in the Anglo/Roman ranks?" Barbara asked.

"They are the Anglo/Roman ranks, everyone on that side is under them." Caitlyn sighed. "All the popular kids from High School are now the popular kids on campus, and in the game."

Barbara smirked, then burst out laughing, "I've never been popular, I'm the weirdo in the corner! So not being noticed by them isn't going to bother me one little bit!"

Caitlyn's mouth dropped open to protest, and then she too was laughing. "Tim's right, you're good for us!"

"I'm glad he thinks so." Barbara laughed.

"So, we're not the in crowd," Caitlyn conceded. "Most of us are just what we are, none of us are going to be wheeler dealers. But we do have fun."

"Have you read this rule book?" Barbara asked.

"No, and I doubt if any of either side is honest, have any of the others." Caitlyn stated emphatically.

"Let me tell you," Barbara stood up and looked at her reflection, holding the Viking tunic up against her, "whoever wrote this, had a good grasp of history. I think they changed things up, so they wouldn't have to play royalties to someone. IT's not a bad concept for a game."

Caitlyn stood behind her, "It started out as a board game when my folks were teens, I heard. Gave competition to that D&D game. Then when LARP's started, it became all the rage. It was going for quite some time when it came to our little burg. It started small, was played in open gyms and in convention centers for a while. Then when Tim joined and got my membership, it moved around looking for a permanent home."

"And this empty mall?" Barbara asked.

"It used to be this really great shopping mall when I was little. I remember going to see Santa there." Caitlyn became nostalgic. "It had three anchor stores, a bunch of fancy boutiques, and some pretty pricey jewelry shops. Then suddenly, bam, it went dead. Everything pulled out."

"That's odd, you say it was doing well?"

Caitlyn nodded again, "My father's firm tried to sue the owners when they reneged on some contracts, and then suddenly they evicted everyone! Big stores and little." She shook her head, "Such a shame, a lot of local people lost jobs."

"So, why are they willing to rent to a game group?" Barbara frowned; it didn't make sense.

"Near as I can figure, someone goofed and rented it to the group long term but couldn't pull out of it. So at least for now, and until we graduate college, the mall belongs to the Conquest of Iron." Caitlyn murmured. "You should have seen it when the game moved in. It was a mess! Several spots in the roof leaked, and there were puddles on the tiles. They didn't take out any of the plantings, and the vines over grew and it was smelly and dirty. I will admit, the retainers came in and did clean up and get the air system up and running again. So, it shouldn't be a total disaster. However, I heard they left the overgrown planters."

Barbara turned from her reflection to her friend, "Danbury is a very interesting place," she said. "This game sounds amazing."

"Don't tell Tim I said this," Caitlyn leaned closer, "it is." She looked at the tunic she was lending to her friend. "I really think this outfit fits you much better than it did me."

"I wish I was as pretty as you are," Barbara confided. "Your red hair, and bright eyes, your height, and your figure..." she looked back at the mirror. "What do I have, a short stocky little body and dark hair and brooding looks."

"You're pretty," Caitlyn said, "you have your own kind of beauty."

"You're a sweet person," Barbara said. "But I'm not a fool, I can see that I'm plain as hay compared to you."

"Beauty can't be eaten with a spoon, my grandmother used to say," Caitlyn advised. "Don't sell yourself short."

"A height joke?" Barbara laughed. "Good one!"

Caitlyn nudged her friend, "With the right cloak, and shods, you're going to look far more authentic than I will."

"I really do apricate your lending the gear." Barbara said.

"Oh, I'm not lending, I'm giving you this stuff," Caitlyn countered. "I have a feeling you're going to make me more active in this gaming group, and if I'm going to sit in the stands, so are you!"

"Giving them to me?" Barbara's voice was full of wonder. "Oh Caitlyn, really?"

"We're friends," Caitlyn said nonchalantly. "That's what friends do; you know that."

Barbara shook her head, "No, I don't," she confessed. "Caitlyn, before you and Tim, I didn't have any friends."

"Oh, come on," Caitlyn said.

"No, listen to me," Barbara touched her hand and pulled her back to sit on the bed again. "When I was little, I was the youngest kid at the convent school. The older girls wanted nothing to do with me, even when I got older and was in classes, I was ostracized." She hadn't shared this with anyone, and the confession felt soul good. "I was different from all the others; I didn't go home. I stayed at the school year-round, and my only constant companions were the nuns. Let me tell you something, they are not good companions for a child, even if they were educators. My only experiences with computers was for schoolwork, I didn't play games because I wasn't allowed to." She tightened her hand hold on Caitlyn's hand. "Your generosity to me is not what I am used to."

Caitlyn's big blue eyes widened. "That's so sad."

"I'm not asking for pity," Barbara assured her, "only understanding when I do things that are not what is the norm." She changed the subject, "I read the rule book, and I'd like to know more about this Character-building aspect."

Caitlyn smiled, "Tim's really the one to talk to about that," she said. "He's got a whole chart listing the people in his clan and what their personal histories are, including my character, who he named."

"You don't like the name he selected?"

"It's rather... plain." Caitlyn said. "He called me Caradoc."

Barbara smiled, "Do you know what it means?" When her friend shook her head, Barbara explained, "It means one who is loved." She smiled, "He declared his love for you for all the gamers to know."

"He did?" Caitlyn blushed, "Why didn't he just tell me."

"He told you," Barbara insisted. "He did it in the language of the old Celts."

"Caitlyn, Tim is here," her mother called from the floor below.

"Don't tell him I didn't know," Caitlyn begged.

"Not a word," Barbara followed her out of the room and down to the kitchen where Tim was being served a cup of hot chocolate.

"Hi," he said. "Did you find outfits?"

"Yes," Caitlyn said taking a seat close to him, "Barbara was wondering if you could help her build a character."

"I already started," he pulled notes out of his pocket, "I have a name, but I wasn't sure you'd like it."

"What do you have?"

"Barra," he said slowly.

Barbara stared, "What did you say?"

"Barra," he repeated.

"That means spear, doesn't it?" Barbara asked, but her mind was going somewhere dark, somewhere she didn't want to go. A memory, and a contradiction.

"You look like a shield maiden," Tim said, and she looked at him. "All fierce and ready to do battle."

Caitlyn frowned, "That's not nice Tim!" she scolded. "A girl doesn't want to be told things like that."

"Not so fast," Barbara countered, "I kind of like it. Barra, a shield maiden." She nodded, "Being from a clan of Celts who are mixed with Norse blood... it makes sense. It feels right."

Caitlyn frowned deeper. "But it's..."

"No," Barbara assured, "it's fine. I like it, Barra. Do we have a clan name?"

Tim looked at Caitlyn in triumph. "We do, it's the Clan of the Smertae."

Barbara leaned back, "Tim, you sly dog you," she said. He smiled broadly.

"What?" Caitlyn asked.

"He named the tribe after an actual tribe of the northern region of Scotland." Barbara said.

Caitlyn stared, "You did?"

He nodded.

"Why do you pretend not to know this stuff," Barbara accused. "The chapters on the Smertae is coming up."

"I don't know it like you do," he countered. "I know the game stuff. The Smertae tribes and clans were easy to figure out. It's the dates and technical stuff I don't pay attention to. I told you, I got in this game for the weapons playing." He moved his arm like he had a sword, "Sharp, pointy things."

Barbara put her head on the table. "Tim!"

"I'm honest," he said. "No one can ever accuse me of not being honest."

She looked up at him, "Okay, Barra of the Smertae," she agreed to. "What is her function?"

"You're not going to like it," he said. "But since you're only a spectator at this event, it shouldn't really matter. We can change things up as you get into the game."

"And you really plan on us getting into the game?" Caitlyn asked.

"Sure, why not, it's a fun game, most of the time." He said.

"Warren won't agree," Caitlyn reminded him.

"What do you mean most of the time?" Barbara asked.

"Some of the guys on the other side, they don't think girls should play." Tim shrugged. "Warren Becket, he thinks the girls should be window dressing. Mostly because the girls on their side ware fancy silks and satins... not exactly accurate, but window dressing."

"I see," Barbara said. "I haven't met this guy, what's he really like?"

"He's a male chauvinist pig," both Tim and Caitlyn chorused.

"Oh, he sounds fun," Barbara quipped. "Okay Tim, how do you see Barra?"

"She's the leader of the Clan's shield maidens, and she's a spell caster." He said.

"You're calling Barbara a witch?" Caitlyn shouted.

"No," Barbara said, "He called me a spell caster, there was more to it in the tribal times." She wasn't disturbed or angry, she was intrigued. "Leader of the shield maidens, I like that." She laughed, "Do I get to read the bones too?"

Tim nodded, eagerly and smiled broadly. Caitlyn stared at the pair of them. "I even have a bag of bones for you to wear on your costume belt."

"This sounds like fun!" Barbara said.

"I think you're both crazy," Caitlyn muttered. "And I'm being dragged along for the ride."

SATURDAY MORNING ARRIVED, again Barbara's roomie hadn't spent the night in her bed. It gave Barbara time and room to spread out to get ready for the day's event. Tim had said he and Caitlyn would pick her up at 9 am. Their group would meet at the south end of the mall before 9:30 when the door would open, and they would be allowed to assemble in their appointed portion of the arena.

She had spent the time since Caitlyn had given her the costume, studying the rule book. Having a near eidetic memory allowed her to keep information fresh in her mind. Having a passion for the bronze through the iron age gave her an excitement at being able to play act even a small part of it. Being included in a Clan gave her a delight she couldn't hide. She could just see Mother Angelica's face. The aging nun would have had a fit. Part of that gave her a deep satisfaction, that and being called Barra again even if only in a game.

By 9 she was dressed and at the dorm building door, waiting for her ride. When Tim's car pulled up to the curb she stepped out of the door and walked with purpose. Tim got out of the car and smiled widely, "I knew this was a great idea! You look fantastic!"

"I feel fantastic," Barbara commented. "Like sheading a snakeskin and becoming myself." She got in the car and greeted Caitlyn. "You look amazing, I love the braid."

"Me," Caitlyn said, "look at you! You're far more realistic looking than I am. I love the way you've adapted the costume!"

"I spent three hours last night in the library looking at re-enactors adaptations." Barbara confessed. "I really wanted to get this right, even if I'm just spending the day sitting and watching!"

"You girls won't be alone in the stands," Tim said. "Some of the other girls, hearing that *you* were coming, decided it was time to come and cheer our side on." He pulled out of the lot and headed onto the county road. "The mall is just outside of town, and each side has its own designated parking and its own areas to roam about in."

"There was talk," Caitlyn added, "about putting up some temporary buildings and scenery, but so far, it's only talk."

"We only get to use the main floor," Tim advised. "We are not allowed in the upper floors. However, we have our own restrooms, and the use of one of the old food courts for meals."

Meals? Barbara wondered if she was supposed to supply her own.

"Mom packed a cooler for us, with meat and cheese and bread." Caitlyn said as if she'd read Barbara's mind. "Tim's mom supplies us with drinks in a sperate cooler."

"Do we share?" Barbara asked.

"Communal," Tim nodded as he drove. "And we try to keep the foods a period as we can. Cold meats, cheeses, breads, that sort of things."

"Fruit of the season," Caitlyn added. "Which one of the others on our team supplies."

"This sounds well thought out," Barbara approved.

"It's not as well planned out as say a *SCA* event," Tim said. "But we're a much smaller group, and they are more established and have more moeny." He explained. "When we get to the mall, we'll met up with the rest of our clan, or at least everyone who's playing today. Not everyone can make every tourney." He said. "We'll put our food in the court and do set up. We put up pikes and shields and banners to designate our area, just as the opponents do. Then we do a quick strategy meeting."

"Who starts the aggression?" Barbara inquired.

"Warren," again the pair in the front seat said in unison.

"This should be interesting," Barbara said settling back for the rest of the short ride to the mall. She enjoyed the rolling countryside of her new hometown and outlying area. There was something so invigorating about it. After being cooped up for years, never allowed outside of the cloister garden of the convent schools, she felt like she could really breath.

The mall was sprawling, from the outside it looked only a bit worn and dated. Had she not known it was closed for business, she would have expected to see cars pulling in with willing shoppers. The grounds looked as if they had been let go, but it was clean and not dilapidated. Seeing a patrol car, she wondered if the town or the corporation payed for security.

There were cars parked in the lot area that Tim pulled toward. "I see Bill got his dad's van," he commented.

"Some of the guys don't like to haul their gear," Caitlyn commented. "Tim here wouldn't let anyone else touch his stuff."

"I paid more," he said. "Some of them had older brothers who played this game, and they have hand me down gear. I didn't, my older brother was a football player, not a history nut."

"How is it you didn't get into organized sports?" Barbara asked.

"Couldn't compete with my older brother," Tim answered. "But I like this stuff better anyway. Give me a shield and a blade or an axe and I'm a happy man." He parked his car. "You should see me on a horse in a joust."

SIGN OF THE RAVEN

One of the young men coming toward the car, Barbara recognized from the study group. "You didn't tell me Dan was part of the game."

"You're going to see nearly every member of the study group," Tim advised. "And not everyone is on our team, one or two are on the other side."

With the boys doing the lugging of the coolers and the equipment, the girls moved into the mall and headed to the food courtyard where they set up 'camp'. Banners were strung, pikes were placed, and shields were displayed.

The actual playing field was the area between food courts, north and south. North belonging to the Anglo/Romans, south belonging to the Smertae. Barbara took a moment to acquaint herself with the layout. While the staircases remained, where there had been escalators was open space, blocked off on the upper level. She looked up at the upper level of the mall, it was dark and murky compared to the open area with the atrium glass above. There were lights on here in the lower level, but even so, some of the areas were also murky. She had to admit, it had ambiance.

Storefronts had been boarded up, and there were no open areas off the main floorplan. Caitlyn had pointed out the restrooms off the food court. Barbara noted that someone had brought in bales of hay to outline the spectator areas. The boys sang a song of battle while setting up, and on the chorus the girls joined in. By the time they finished, even Barbara was singing "How many of them can we make die?"

The other side was less congenial as they set up. They worked without song and seemed to be ignoring the Smertae completely. Except they were not really ignoring them, several glared at the sounds of voices in disdain. Caitlyn's and Tim's description of the young women in that group was all too actuate. They were window dressing. They didn't even help with setting up the food court but stood by like mannequins as younger men of that group set things up as wanted. Even their faces were stoic and motionless. They didn't look happy about being there, they looked apprehensive at best, and moved when ordered by the young men into place. They even sat like mannequins, joyless and expressionless.

"They have their own pages?" Barbara whispered to Caitlyn who nodded sadly.

Barbara recognized one of the girls seated, she was Dawn Martin, a pretty, bright blond with skin like cream. She was dressed in blue satins and gold trim. Her eyes never drifted off the young man who was ordering others about.

"And that must be Warren Becket," Barbara said to herself.

Tim let go of a long low whistle, and Barbara looked at him. His face held concern. "What are they doing here?" he asked one of the boys setting up.

The other looked and frowned, "Damned if I know, they were here when we got here."

"Who are *they*," Barbara asked Tim.

"Board members for the region," Tim explained as he looked at the official looking men who were costumed. "The game has chapters all over, each region has its own board who answers to the corporate board. They only show up if there's a problem or a convention." He shook his head, "I didn't invite them, and from the look on Warren's face, he didn't either."

"Could they mean trouble?" Barbara asked.

"Could, but let's not beg trouble." Tim advised, "It could be just one of their official look-sees."

"Look-see?" Barbara raised a brow. "Really?" She looked at the men, who were a little older than the main game players of the area. One stood out, he was tall, lean, and brooding, however, he didn't wear a costume of a knight like other board members, but rather that of a Viking warlord. His leather had been embossed with the symbols of Oden. His features were chiseled, strong and full of character. He wasn't pretty like Warren, nonetheless he was far more commanding.

And if she were any judge, he didn't like Warren. He didn't appear to like anyone, not even the other members of the board, whom he stood apart from purposefully. He stood with his arms crossed, a scowl on that handsome face. There was impatience written on the chiseled features.

She was surprised when he shifted his gaze when his dark brooding eyes met hers. Suddenly there was a spark in his eyes, a recognition she'd not gained from anyone else. His arms slowly dropped to his side and he appeared to be holding his breath as his head cocked to one side. Barbara turned away, not intending to look at him further. Something about him filled her with excitement and dread in the same instant. Whoever he was, she had a feeling things were about to get very tense.

Caitlyn had moved to their spectators stand with some of the other girls, she had taken a drop spindle out of a leather pouch. Another girl held a hand loom and was weaving a long scarf like length of fabric. Each of the girls had hand work and were talking quietly among themselves. Barbara, being new to the group didn't have a task to work on and began to pace the length of the stand keeping an eye on the field and the warriors who were defending territory. Every now and again she looked up at the upper level where the board had gathered on one of the stair platforms. The six men were observing the battle play and discussing something between themselves.

When lunch was called, the battle was halted, it was clear that the Anglo side seemed to have an edge on the Celtic Norsemen. The boys returned to the safety of the food court, dripping in sweat, looking a bit the worse for wear. It amazed Barbara, their team seemed happy, not at all in despair. She glanced over at the opposite side, in their food court, one would have thought that they were losing by their attitudes. The boys were ordering the pages and the young women about with harsh and angry words.

Barbara looked up at the platform, expecting it to be empty. The Viking warlord was gazing down at her, amused. He was leaning on the rail, a wisp of a smile playing at the corner of his lips. He inclined his head toward her; she returned the gesture on a whim. His smile became a smirk, not haughty but rather charming as it even made his eyes look more animated. He only looked away when he was distracted by something going on in the opposition's 'camp'. The smirk faded.

She heard the commotion as well and turned to look. Warren was ordering people about and was clearly not happy about something. She could only guess what it was. She caught him looking their way, and the hair on the back of her neck stood up. He was up to something, and it wasn't going to be good. Some inner instinct told her to look about, make sure she knew what was at hand. She allowed the implements of war that decorated their stand to be etched into her mind. She knew placement of each weapon and made her choice.

After a rest period, the battle resumed, and instantly became heated. Warren had given orders; they were being followed. Not being familiar with the game, but with the rules of the game, Barbara could see that Warren was pressing an advantage. He was pushing their team back to the 'territory' they had emerged from. More than that, he was pushing the battle back toward *their* spectator stand. When suddenly, without warning, Warren headed around and over the boundary and into the stand. He bolted over the bale of hay and was upon Caitlyn who instinctively raised her arms to protect herself. She screamed out in real pain as the rattan sword connected with her arm, and Barbara heard bones crunch.

Barbara bolted into action as Warren came over the hay wall. She grabbed up the pike she was standing closest too and swung it with precision. Connecting with the back of Warren's knees, forcing him to collapse. Having toppled him, she put the pike at his neck.

"Foul!" Warren shouted. "Foul on the Smertae!" He made a move to get up, but Barbara had placed a foot on his chest. "Let me up you stupid slut!" he cursed. "Back off!"

SIGN OF THE RAVEN

Hearing the slur, she pushed him down with her foot harder. "One more word," she warned, "and it will be your last."

Warren's eyes opened in wide anger, but he kept his mouth shut until the board members arrived. "Get this bitch off me," he demanded.

"Shut up, dead man." Barbara ordered. "You've no say."

"You can't talk to me that way," Warren countered in anger, "You're not even a member of the game."

"You made me a member," she accused back.

Warren stared at her in disbelieve. "No, I did not, you're crazy."

"The moment you bolted that boundary, you dragged everyone in this viewing stand into the playing field." She added, "It's in the rules."

"Where," he challenged, not caring that the board members were there.

"You didn't even read the rules, did you?" she challenged. "It's on page sixty-eight, paragraph three."

"She's right," the man who had been watching her said, his voice was deep, and calm. "It's in the rules."

Barbara, emboldened went on, "In accordance with the rules, I am now in active play and have killed you for attacking our lodge." She looked at Caitlyn who was turning very pale, "You'd better have a paramedic check her." She said to the man from the board, who moved quickly to the injured girl. "I heard bones crunch."

"I didn't hit her that hard," Warren objected.

"This looks like a fracture," the stranger said. "Call the paramedics, and have an ambulance brought." He shouted to another member of the board who took a cell phone out of his pouch on his belt.

Warren moved, and Barbara shoved him down flat with her foot. "As the victor of this unplanned attack, I claim his helm, his sword, his shield and his cloak." She announced.

"You're not even a member," Warren objected. "You can't claim anything!"

"Yes, she is," Tim said removing his leather face protector, "I bought her a membership on Friday. Ask Bentley." He shrugged at Barbara, "I figured if you got active so would Caiti." He moved to his wounded girlfriend. "I'm sorry honey, I shouldn't have asked you to come."

"It's not your fault," Barbara disagreed, "It's Warren's."

The Viking warlord nodded, "The take down was fair, and by the rules, the attack on the stand was not." He turned to Barbara, "You and the rest of the ladies in this stand are now in active play."

"That means the girls in his stand are also, right?" Barbara inquired.

"Yes," he answered. "Anything else you'd like to know?"

Barbara picked up Warren's shield, slapped his rattan sword against it. "Shield Maidens," she shouted. The other girls in the stand also picked up shields and swords that had decorated the stand. Barbara looked down at the girls in the other stand with deer in the headlight stares, "How many of them can we make die?" She shouted.

CAITLYN WAS TAKEN TO the hospital; Warren was forced to sit out the rest of the tourney, and not in his own stand but in the stand of the Celts. By the time Caitlyn came back with one of the board members, Barbara and her shield maidens had captured the other stand and had taken prisoners. For the first time in three years, the Anglo/Romans of this branch of the game were defeated. Barbara noticed a lot of shields that didn't belong to the group being displayed on their stand. She ordered them confiscated and locked up in the equipment locker that the boys were packing.

Warren stalked over to her, "I'll take my stuff now, if you don't mind." He snarled.

"Nope," Barbara denied his request.

"What do you mean, nope?"

SIGN OF THE RAVEN

She looked at him, "Until the Tourney is over, which is three months from now, your belongings are my trophies. Your stand, or castle if you like, is mine, your women are now mine. You should have read the rules."

Warren turned on Dawn, "I asked you to do one lousy thing," he shouted. "Keep control of the stand; you couldn't even do that..." He pointed a finger in her face threateningly.

Dawn's face blanched, and Barbara was fearful he was about to do her some harm. She swung the rattan sword to the back of Warren's knees and felled him again. When he collapsed, she grabbed hold of his hair and shouted in his face. "If you ever threaten that girl again, Warren Becket, I'm going to make you sorry you were ever born. I will not tolerate you bullying her or any other girl here! In play or at school! The only person you have to blame for losing is yourself!"

One of Warren's teammates was about to come to his aid, but the Viking stopped him, "She's got this." He said.

Warren's eyes opened and he looked over at Dawn. "I wouldn't bully her," he said in shock. "I... didn't..."

"You just did," Barbara pointed out. "And I'll bet it's not the first time you big, spoiled brat. You called me by a slur when I felled you, and you don't even know me!"

Warren's breath came fast, "I... I..."

"Look at her, she's scared of you." Barbara turned his head forcefully. "She's too good for the likes of you!" She released his hair and moved to Dawn. "You don't ever have to be afraid of him again." Barbara had known bullies, bigger and badder than Warren, and because she knew what real bullies could do, she wasn't about to let it happen right in front of her. Something about the game had empowered her.

Warren crawled up to his knees, "Wait," he begged. "I never meant to scare her... I was just angry...I..."

Dawn had tears in her eyes. Barbara looked at the rest of the young men on the Anglo team. "Nothing but a bunch of spoiled brats and bullies, the lot of you. And you've been getting away with it for years, well no more!" She pointed at the group gathered, "It ends now."

Warren stood up, "Dawn, honey, you know I'd never hurt you."

"Like you never meant to hurt Caitlyn," Barbara scowled, "Well you broke her arm, Warren."

Warren was speechless for a moment, "I didn't mean to... I only wanted to..."

"To what? Show off? Take the stand and us as your trophies? Prove to the board that you're the better team because you're the Anglos?" Barbara accused.

The Viking cocked a brow and looked, waiting for an answer.

Warren looked over at the Viking. "Damn." He said quietly, "That's exactly what I was doing." He looked then at Dawn, "Baby, I'm sorry... I let this game get out of hand. I never meant to bully you, or them." He turned to Barbara. "You're right, I'm just a big, spoiled brat used to getting my way. I'm sorry, I had no right to call you out of your name, especially since I don't even know it."

The Viking smirked, "You could make him sit in your stand for the rest of the series," he suggested. "An effigy of your winning; or you could auction him off with the slaves you won today."

"These women are not slaves; they are now *my* banner women." Barbara countered hotly, angry at the Viking for suggesting she enslave the others. "As for Warren... we'll see."

He smiled slyly, "As you wish, my Lady."

Warren swallowed, thought through his options, and said, "I bow to the will of the Shield Maiden."

Chapter 3.

A week after her first mall battle, Barbara heard someone calling out as she walked down the steps of the college's library. She was bundled up against the wind and thought she was mistaken until she heard the voice shouting.

"Barb! Hey, Barb! Wait up!"

She turned to see who was calling, and to her utter surprise, it was Warren Becket. He and Dawn were running down the quad steps to catch up to her. He reached out a hand and touched her shoulder, as if he and she were old time, longtime friends. He was smiling, "Didn't you hear me calling?" he asked with a grin.

"No one ever called me Barb, expect Tim and only one time," she said shyly. "I'm not used to being called to."

"Well, you're going to hear it a lot from now on," he promised. "I saw you in there," he thumbed back at the building behind them, "and I wanted to make sure we talked."

"Oh? I wasn't aware we had a class together." She couldn't believe this was the same young man who only a week ago had called her a slut without even knowing her. "What did you want to talk about?"

"The Winter Solstice Ball, of course," he said as if it were a given. "You are coming, aren't you?"

Barbara blinked, "The what?"

"Honey, she's not from here." Dawn shook her head at Warren, "The Winter Solstice Ball," she repeated, "It used to be the Christmas Ball until the college went all PC." She explained. "It's only the biggest social event of the season." She too was smiling at Barbara. "You really have to come! Everyone in the game will be there! We all go dressed in our best fancy costumes."

"Oh," Barbara didn't know how to react, "This is the first I've heard of it."

"I was afraid of that," Warren said taking a flyer out of his notebook. "These just came out today, I grabbed one of these for you," he said handing it to her. "It's going to be held at Jubilee Park, that's a fancy banquet hall." He added, "If you need a ride or anything, I hope you'll let me know."

Barbara looked up from the page, "Are you trying to make up to me?" she asked with suspicion.

"Maybe a bit," he admitted. "I felt like such a jerk after what happened. I had no idea I had been behaving so badly. No one ever called me on it."

"Ever wonder why?" She asked directly.

"Oh, I know why," he nodded, "but it only sunk in after you knocked me down the second time." He shrugged, "I'm not really such a bad guy. I'd like the chance to prove it. I'd like us to be friends."

"Why?"

"Because you're the first girl to ever knock some sense into him," Dawn said.

Warren nodded. "She's right. You see, Barb, because my family is rich, everyone let me get away with all kinds of things. You're the first girl to call me out on it." He snorted, "And if you think I'm bad, you should have seen the shit my older brother's got into. I'm nothing compared to them!"

"So, you're the baby of the family, as well as coming from one of the founding families," she surmised. "I still don't see a reason for us to be friends," she handed the flyer back.

"On the surface, no." He agreed. "But you're a smart girl, a strong person who isn't afraid of me or any of the other big-name people around here. Now, I don't think that it's just that you're new here." He explained. "I'm not stupid, vein and spoiled, but not stupid," he added. "I know that you're going to be a force to contend with, and I know when I need to switch sides."

"I'm not giving back the helm," Barbara said flatly. "I won it and the rest of your gear fair and square."

Warren laughed, "I'm not asking you to."

SIGN OF THE RAVEN

"What are you asking?" She demanded.

"I'm asking for a chance to prove that I'm an okay person." He said. "I'll even play the display for you at events and take my punishment like a man. Not just because the members of the board saw me being an ass, but because you're right and it's in the rules." He guffawed, "I finally read the rule book."

Dawn took the flyer and handed it back to Barbara, "For far too long," she said, "the Anglo/Roman fraction of the game has pulled this we are better than you, shit around this town. Not everyone who plays the game is like that. The other branches are not like this one."

Barbara looked at the flyer. "You say everyone attends?" She wondered why Caitlyn hadn't told her about this.

"Give it some thought," Warren suggested. "Get to know everyone off the battlefield. Give us a chance, we're really an okay crowd."

"I'll think about it," Barbara promised.

"Great," Warren said. "If you need anything, let me know!" He looked at the clock tower on the building behind them. "Got to run, I'll be late for the commerce class. See you!"

Barbara tucked the flyer into her books and headed to her next class. When she arrived, Caitlyn was already there. Her arm was in a sling and she was having trouble getting her book on the desk.

"Let me help you," Barbara offered. She took the book out of the case and put it on the long table in front of them.

"Thanks, this sling is a pain in the ass." Caitlyn complained.

"How long will you be in it?" Barbara took her seat beside her.

"Six weeks," Caitlyn complained. "It's going to be a drag." She leaned back. "Barbara, the flyers just came out for an event I wanted to tell you about. The Winter Solstice Ball," she said, matter of factly. "It's sort of a big deal here about," she said, and looked down at her sling. "This is going to make my choice of dress less fun."

"Warren stopped me at the Library with this," she pulled out the flyer. "He said he wanted to make sure I know about it."

Caitlyn nodded, "He would." She didn't seem to be taken aback by the news. "The Ball is sort of the height of the winter social events around here. Attendance is open to seniors from the high school now, but it wasn't always that way. It used to be only open to the college attendees." Caitlyn explained. "You're not from here, so you wouldn't know about the ins and outs of this thing."

"Ins and outs?" Barbara questioned helping her friend to sit and taking a seat beside her.

Caitlyn nodded, "Most of the college students attend in black tie." Caitlyn expounded. "Even some of the girls go out and get tuxes." She didn't sound impressed. "A few years ago, when it was re-designated the Solstice Ball, the members of the Conquest game started attending in fancy court dress. Trying to make it a statement."

"Did you?"

She nodded, "Tim took me last year when we were seniors, and yes we came in fancy costumes."

"So, it's a couples thing," Barbara murmured, feeling like she was going to have to decline.

"No," Caitlyn said. "I mean couples attend, but it's open invitation."

"You look uncomfortable," Barbara studied her, "is that painful?"

"A little," Caitlyn admitted. "I can't get used to this sling, and it's hard to do the simplest of things, like getting dressed and undressed."

"I'm so sorry you got hurt," Barbara said.

"I wanted to thank you," Caitlyn whispered. "For acting so quickly and getting Warren off me." She rubbed her sore arm. "The doctor said it would have been much worse than a fracture if he'd hit me again."

"I only did what was natural," Barbara said. "I didn't even think."

"You did more than save me," Caitlyn acknowledged. "You won for our side and took the Anglo/Roman castle with a *team of girls*." She looked at Barbara, her face a mask of seriousness. "Have you any idea of what you've done?"

"No."

SIGN OF THE RAVEN

"You brought *girls* into the active game."

Barbara shrugged. "So?"

"It's never been done, at least, not here." Caitlyn said. "I'm not sure if its good or bad."

"Are you mad at me?" Barbara asked.

Shaking her head side to side, Caitlyn answered. "No. I'm scared."

"I'll drop out of the game," Barbara said.

"No," Caitlyn disagreed. "They won't let you, even if you wanted to. And I don't want you to drop out."

"What do you want?"

"I want you to be careful," Caitlyn advised. "You did something no one ever has, but I don't want you to just trust on face value the friendships being offered. I don't trust Warren and the rest of the Anglo boys."

"I can understand why you wouldn't," Barbara said. "I have my own misgivings of him."

"Just be careful." Caitlyn begged. "The girls are alright, just uptight, but even they might loosen up with you running the shield maidens."

"I will be careful." She looked at the flyer. "Are you going to this?"

"Tim is getting the tickets today," Caitlyn nodded, "He's getting one for you too." She divulged.

"He doesn't have to," Barbara protested.

"He wants to, and I think he's right," Caitlyn smiled. "You need to attend, and you should be with us, we're a trio now."

Barbara knew class would start soon, "Caitlyn, I don't have a fancy gown." She reminded her. "What I wore last week to the tourney, you gave me."

Caitlyn's mouth dropped open, "OH, Barbara, you must think I'm a moron."

"No, I think you forget I'm not from here, and that I don't have a normal life."

Caitlyn couldn't retort as the instructor came in and class began. When class ended, she turned to Barbara. "I'm an idiot," she said. "I meant to start with, my mother wondered if you'd like to make your gown at our house."

"Make my gown?" Barbara blinked. "Caitlyn, I don't know how to sew."

Caitlyn blinked, "What did those nuns teach you?"

"Only what they had to," Barbara shot back, then laughed. "Which wasn't a lot."

Her friend shook her head, "Look, mom has patterns, and tons of fabric, and if I can learn to sew anybody can." She stood up and struggled with the book to get it in her case. Barbara put the book back. "Come home with me for supper tonight."

"On short notice, is that fair to your mom?"

"Mom said you are welcome anytime, she says she's adopting you into the family," Caitlyn assured her. "Say you'll come."

"Alright," Barbara agreed. "I'll meet you on the square."

"I'm not driving right now," Caitlyn explained. "This arm is a pain in the ass." She picked up her case sliding it up her good arm. "Tim will drop us off on his way home, and Dad will take you back to the dorms when we're done."

"Sounds good," Barbara made sure Caitlyn had everything. "I'll see you on the green."

CAITLYN'S HOUSE FELT like home to Barbara, or at least what she thought home was supposed to feel like. Snow was falling when Tim drove them home, and the sun was going down. He had a 24-hour Christmas station on and commented several times on how much he loved fresh fallen snow. The farmhouse looked like a picture post card. Snow coming down, house lit up with seasonal lights and smoke curling out of several chimneys. Barbara could see the fresh cords of wood that had been stacked on the porch.

"That's beautiful," Barbara commented as she stepped out of the car and grabbed up Caitlyn's case for her. "It's what all houses should look like in winter. I wish I had the talent to paint something like this."

Caitlyn looked at the house, "I think I take it for granted," she admitted. "Always having had it."

"Don't," warned Barbara. "All too quickly it could be snatched away. I don't really remember the house I lived in with my parents, it's all foggy."

Caitlyn leaned into her, "I feel so bad for you," she whispered.

"Don't," Barbara whispered back. "I'm grateful for what I have now. For you, and Tim... for your family taking me in..."

"You're not little orphan Annie," Caitlyn teased.

"I'd shoo the chickens and brush the crumbs away if that's what your mom and dad needed me to do," Barbara confessed in a serious tone, remembering part of the poem.

Caitlyn giggled, "I'll mention that."

"Do," Barbara giggled as well.

When they entered the house, Mrs. O'Hara had hot tea ready to warm them. "So, what is on the addenda for this evening?" she asked.

"Pattern hunting, and fabric bin diving," Caitlyn said. "Barbara needs a gown for the ball, and we have only two weeks to plan it out."

Mrs. O'Hara looked at Barbara appraisingly, "I think I can save you both a lot of work," she said. "I was going through the bin for Molly earlier, she's got to do an outfit for the Choir's madrigal singers dinner, and I came across something that might work." She walked out of the kitchen and returned a short time later. She put a pattern on the table, in front of Barbara. "I saw this and thought of you."

The pattern was old, the envelop had yellowed with age. It was a gown that looked like a mixture of ages, fantasy, and reality, and of purposes. The under-gown was draped down from the shoulders, with ornamental metal fasteners. The long sleeve was open, caught here and there with smaller bits of metal, then cascaded down to nearly the floor. Over this was an over gown that looked more Celtic with lacing and knotwork trim, belted with embossed leather.

"I can't even sew a button," Barbara said, "I wouldn't begin to know how to do this." She confessed, "And this belted thing... and then there's the fabric and the notions." She shook her head, "This is way over me."

"Nonsense." Mrs. O'Hara bragged. "If I can teach Caitlyn to sew, I can teach you. We can whip this up in no time at all. One Saturday! I promise." She leaned on the table, "And you'd be doing me a favor getting rid of some of the stash of fabric I've accumulated. I don't know what I was thinking buying and stashing all that fabric."

"Won't you be busy making Caitlyn's dress, and Molly's?" Barbara asked.

"Caitlyn's dress was finished in August," Mrs. O'Hara countered, "but don't tell Tim, he thinks we're still designing it. I just need to make an adjustment for her sling. As for Molly, she's doing her own sewing, I'm just supervising."

"I would like to learn to sew," Barbara said quietly, "I think it's a good skill to have." She looked once more at the pattern, "But this belt..."

"It's a waist chinch," Mrs. O'Hara corrected. "Decorative mostly." She turned the pattern towards her, "I think we can work the leather into the surcoat and save ourselves a lot of trouble. It's not like you're needing it to be functional, there's not an ounce of fat on you." She tapped her fingers. "I've got some embossed light weight leather up in the attic, we can make little side panels and it will give the right look."

"You're not going to take no, are you?" Barbara conceded.

"Hadn't planned to, no." Mrs. O'Hara agreed. "After dinner, you and Caiti go up to the fabric bin, dig in and find what we need. I've got some wonderful buttons up there that will work for the fasteners with loops."

Barbara wanted to cry, overjoyed at such generosity. "I don't know how to thank you."

"Don't try," Caitlyn's mother said. "I owe you, for rescuing Caiti here."

"Alright, let's give it a try," Barbara agreed. "I really would like to learn to sew."

AFTER DINNER, WHILE the younger siblings were doing homework, Caitlyn and Barbara went up to the sewing room on the second floor. They entered the attic through a door that hid the stairs.

"This was a storage room when we moved in," Caitlyn explained, "Mom converted it to the sewing room, and stashed her treasury of fabric up here." She led the way. The attic was chilly, but not so cold that it was uncomfortable. The lights were spaced so that there were no dark corners, the lights quickly warmed the space.

"This is amazing." Barbara said.

"We all used to play up here while mom would sew," Caitlyn reminisced. "Over there is where the decorations for Christmas are kept when they are not in use, and over on this side, mom's stash. And in that wardrobe is some of our outgrown costumes."

There were several cabinets, made of cedar, inside which were bolts of fabric. "She has them marked off by type, wool, silk, satin, velvets..." She motioned to a drawer, "Trims are in there, and in the drawer under it, buttons. I bet she's got at least a million buttons. Every shape, size and material." Caitlyn bragged. She handed Barbara the list of suggestions her mom had written down. "For the under gown, silk or gauze. You'll find them in the first cabinet."

Barbara nodded and opened the doors. "What color?"

"Mom suggested cream or peach." Caitlyn took a seat, "I'd say cream, it's a bit more in keeping with the accuracy. Mom doesn't care about that, but I think you and I do."

"We're straying enough off accuracy and authenticity as it is," Barbara agreed. "Cream," she pulled out two bolts one gauze, one silk. "Gauze if you ask me."

"Pull a foot off each and let's see how it moves," Caitlyn suggested, then watched. "Gauze," she agreed. "Put it here, and we'll get the rest of our fabrics after you put the silk back."

"What's next?" Barbara looked at the list, "Your mom suggested we look at the upholstery material for the surcoat." Barbara looked over at Caitlyn, skeptically. "Upholstery?"

Caitlyn nodded, not surprised. "She picked up a bunch of bolt ends when the mall's upholstery and curtain guy went out of business. God only knows what you'll find in there, but if she suggested it, she knows."

Again, Barbara opened the labeled door of one of the cabinets to be greeted by a myriad of colors and patterns. One stood out, "I think I've found what she was thinking about." She pulled the bolt end and showed it to Caitlyn.

"Oh yeah," Caitlyn agreed, "That is so you!" She patted the other bolt. "Put it here, and we'll look for the leather panels she wants us to use and the notions. There's a basket on that shelf, put all the trims and findings and threads in there to carry."

Half an hour later, Caitlyn carried the basket with her good arm, while Barbara carried the bolts. Mrs. O'Hara was in the sewing room, setting up a dress form that had dials on it. "Oh good," she said. "you found the tapestry fabric I was thinking would work. What do you think?"

"I think it goes with the gauze like it was made for it," Barbara agreed. "I'm still not sure about that leather," she added.

"Think of the leather as applique." Mrs. O'Hara suggested. "Decorative, not functional."

Barbara placed the bolts on the cutting table. "I wish the nuns had taught me to sew," she complained. "One would think they would have."

"Did they have sewing classes in your school?" Caitlyn asked.

"No, but they did teach a couple of the girls to do embroidery and some crewel work when they needed new kneelers in the chapel." Barbara remembered, "I wasn't one of them."

"Why not?" Mrs. O'Hara asked innocently.

"Because Mother Angelica considered me a demon spawn," Barbara said, "she didn't want anything I touched in her chapel."

Mrs. O'Hara listened, then laughed, "Oh, Barbara!"

"I'm serious."

Mrs. O'Hara nodded, "I know, that's what makes it so funny." She continued to laugh. She held a handout to her daughter's friend, "Well, don't worry, if I can teach Caitlyn, I can teach you."

BARBARA WAS STAYING at the O'Hara house for the winter break. Tim was to pick them up for the dinner dance. Caitlyn and Barbara worked on each other's hair, and Caitlyn gave Barbara cosmetic tips. Barbara was still unsure of what she was doing and was glad she had the help. By the time Mrs. O'Hara called to them that Tim had arrived, they were both ready.

Caitlyn lent a cloak to Barbara for the occasion, as she said it would be too much for Barbara to wear the cloak she'd won from Warren. While it was a very warm garment, Barbara shook all the way over to the venue. "I shouldn't have come," she muttered to herself in the back seat.

"A touch of nerves, Babs?" Tim asked as he pulled into the lot.

"More than a touch," she confessed, ignoring the nickname. "I don't know why I'm even here."

Caitlyn looked back at her, "Why do you say that?"

"I can't dance," she blurted out. Tim and Caitlyn exchanged a look and then both burst out laughing. "It's not funny," Barbara said before she too burst into laughter.

The venue had been decorated to resemble a winter wonderland. There were decorations from all over the world, celebrating as many traditions as possible. In the gallery above, a small but decent orchestra played. Tim had taken their cloaks to be checked and Caitlyn and Barbara waited for him in the lobby.

"There they are," Barbara heard Warren call out, "Hey Barb! You made it!" He and Dawn and several other of the Anglo/Roman group came toward them. "They have our entire group seated together in the same section! They mixed the tables so there's equal numbers of each side at each table."

"Whose idea was that?" Barbara inquired, thinking it was Warren's.

"Mine," a voice behind her said. She turned to see the Viking warlord in a magnificent assemble. "I thought it was time for both sides to remember it's just a game and that they need to be more social." He moved toward Barbara. "Trey Lochwood," he said extending a hand to her. "We were never properly introduced."

"Barbara Gowan," she answered placing her hand in his. His fingers closed about her hand, she expected him to shank her hand and release it. Instead he smoothly he tucked her hand into his elbow.

"I hope you don't mind," he said cordially, "I've asked to be seated at your table as your dinner partner." He added. "I was informed you didn't have a date for this evening."

"You're always welcomed at our table," Warren said taking a lead.

Tim stared at Warren, then smiled at Lochwood, "We'd be most happy to play your host this evening."

Warren looked at Tim, and said, "I meant we." He assured his opponent. "Didn't I say we?"

Tim shook his head, "You said our, and made it sound like *mine*."

Warren rolled his eyes, "Sorry."

Lochwood smiled down at Barbara, "I hope it's alright with you."

"Its fine," she said politely. "I have only one question. Is this an official visit by a board member?"

SIGN OF THE RAVEN

He patted the hand in the crook of his arm, "More of an unofficial friendly visit." He assured her. "I must say, I was very impress with your knowledge of our rules." He glanced at Warren and Tim both with dark eyes, "Some of our members don't seem to be aware of the rules, or they haven't cared very much about them."

"That must be frustrating for the officials." She agreed.

"The game is supposed to be friendly competition, not all out war," He was looking at Warren with intent.

"You're a bit young to be an official, aren't you?" She asked as they began to walk to the table. He was older than her friends, but not by much.

"I've been part of this game since I was a boy," he confessed. "My grandfather started it as a board game to teach my father and uncles about history and geography. It worked so well with them, that they introduced it to their classmates, and the company was started. My father and his brother David switched it up to live action when they took over the running of the company while they were in college. There's still a board game, but now there's also a computer version. When my brothers and I came along, we got into the live action play. I worked my way up to the board; my father didn't just hand me the job."

Barbara liked what she was hearing, "So you understand the ins and outs of the game, and you see some of the problems that we're having." She commented as she took the seat reserved for her, in her Game name of Barra.

"I do," he said taking the seat beside her, his card read Skald Trygve. "Although I admit, Danbury is the area with the most contention between players." He looked at Warren and Tim, "I am mystified as to why. You all seem to be reasonable people."

Barbara held up her hands, "I'm an outsider," she confessed. "I only came to Danbury to attend the college, thanks to a scholarship. I make no claim at being reasonable."

"As a newcomer," he said changing her words a bit, "you might have insights that I don't have. I'm too close to the problems, I grew up near here, yet even I don't understand what is going on here with this branch."

"From what I've been told, it goes back to when this area was part of the Colonies." Barbara said without reservation. "The haves, the have-nots and the up and coming."

Trey listened, his eyes never leaving her face. "You're serious." He said calmly, not entirely surprised.

"I am," she nodded. "But you have only to ask these two." She motioned to Tim and Warren who were both staring at her.

"Hey," Tim said defensively. "Don't pick on us."

"It's not a mark against you personally," Barbara said. "But both you and Warren are constantly in competition over nothing. And I have a feeling you've known each other all your lives." She directed her conversation at Warren, "You knew better than to attack the viewing stand, yet you threw caution to the wind, trying to impress the board members present."

Warren squirmed, "I think you're being a bit hard on us." He said to Barbara. "Maybe we are a bit overzealous on my team." He was trying to downplay his embarrassment.

"A bit?" she countered, then pointed at the sling on Caitlyn's arm. "You damn near broke her bones, as it is it's fractured."

Caitlyn lifted the sling for emphasis. "Hello!"

Warren looked at Caitlyn, "I didn't mean..." he said apologetically.

"Didn't you?" Dawn argued, joining the conversation. "Do you remember what you said to us during set up?"

Warren blanched.

Trey smirked, "OH you are so good at getting a conversation going," he said to Barbara. "Had I known this was going to be so lively..." He leaned on an elbow, "Go on."

SIGN OF THE RAVEN

"Tim told me he got into this for the weapons," Barbara pointed out. "That most of the guys in our clan team were into it for the weapons and the pretend war. Warren here, obviously is the same; no one got in it for the love of history except maybe some of the girls, and I'm not sure about them." She turned her attentions on Warren again, "I observed all the shields and helms you've collected and displayed on your fortress wall. What happened to their original owners?"

"That's what the game is about, winning." Warren defended his trophies.

"That's not what the game is about, that's only a side perk," Trey argued. "The game was supposed to give modern people a view of the past. Of what it took to build a civilization so that we don't destroy the one we've inherited."

The severs began to move about the room, delivering the meal. Other tables didn't seem to be having as living a discussion as was going on at the table Barbara was seated at.

"I'll ask again," Barbara said to Warren, "What happened to their owners?"

Warren blinked, "I don't know." He admitted. "I guess they stopped coming..." He hunched forward, muttering something under his breath. "They didn't like losing."

"Do you even care how the other members of *our team* feel about how *you* treat us?" Dawn asked Warren who stared at her in surprise. "The younger boys who are pages want to quit, because you never let them near the battlefield, you order them about like slaves. The girls are sick of being window dressing. I mean really, look at how you and the other boys demand we dressed." She turned in her seat, "You want to know why it was so easy for Barbara here to conquer the castle? I'll tell you why, you never once bothered to teach any of us girls how to defend it!"

Trey leaned back in his seat, "The so-called viewing stands were never intended to be inactive; they are not in other areas, only here. Other groups have the women on teams, as active members!"

"Their shield maidens knew how to use their weapons, rather than us getting hurt, like you hurt Caiti, we surrendered. Look at how you boys demanded we dress. Silks and satins and velvets and veils, we look like overdressed cows, it's not even time accurate." Dawn shook her head, "I'm in class with Barbara, and I've listened to her discuss the workings of fortresses at that time. This fantasy dress-up is not the way the real castle inhabitants dressed, women back then had their own daggers, and some carried swords!"

Trey winked at Barbara, "Now this is progress." He leaned on the table with both arms, "Warren, the way you've out fitted your warriors is about two centuries later than where you're playing."

"It is?" Warren stared. "But we went through the authorized venders."

"Yours isn't the only branch of the game that has gotten off the timeline." Trey stated, "But you have to realize that your group has gotten out of hand. The other branches don't even want to do tourneys with you. The reason we were at the tourney the week after Thanksgiving is because there were complaints against your branch."

Warren looked at Tim, "I thought your side complained because we kept beating you up."

"Why would we, we were having fun," Tim countered. "I thought it was just a routine visit."

Warren put his elbows on the table, on either side of his plate and rested his face in his hands. "Oh, for the love of God."

"Routine?" Trey countered, "When have you ever had three members of the board show up unannounced?"

"I never gave it a thought," Tim said. "The only reason our girls have been sitting in the viewing stand, is Warren said his girls wouldn't take part in the fight. If his girls wouldn't, ours couldn't."

"You did?" Dawn demanded. "You never said we had a choice!"

"I didn't think you'd want to go hand to hand with one of them," Warren pointed to Caitlyn.

"What?" Caitlyn looked at him with daggers, "just what does that mean Warren Becket? Are you suggesting that I'm not as good as Dawn?"

"That's not what I said," he got defensive.

"Yes, it is," Dawn snitched. "You think that because I live in a big house in town, I'm better. But Caitlyn's father is higher up in the same firm than my dad is."

"Warren, you're a snob," Caitlyn accused. "Just because the Becket family is one of the oldest in Danbury."

Warren opened his mouth, then shut it with a snap. He took a deep breath.

Trey held a hand up, "This is why we needed to be there," he suggested. "To get to the bottom of what is going on in your branch. I hate to say this Warren, but your side, the Anglo/Roman side, has segregated it's self away from the principals of the game. Making it impossible to have tourneys with other branches."

"And it's my fault?" Warren asked.

"To a degree," Barbara said. "You're the current leader, and the rest of the boys on your team follow you."

Warren turned to Tim, "Do you think I'm a snob?"

"I never gave it the kind of thought that maybe I should have," he confessed. "See, I was having fun, even if I was getting beaten up. It's like Barbara said, I got in this game for the weapons." He patted Warren on the back, "So, no, I don't think you're a snob. One hell of a fighter, but not a snob."

Warren sighed, "Maybe we did go overboard with our attacks, and maybe we did use the weapons a bit harder than was necessary."

"You demanded your equipment back," Barbara pointed out. "Yet you never returned the so-called *trophies* you've won, I'll bet you never even offered. You just let the others quit and kept their belongings."

"You pushed other players out of the game all together," Dawn accused. "Now some of our pages want to quit, a lot of your *knights* are sick of the way you order them about. They are not having fun anymore!"

Warren sunk down in his chair. "Do you want me to resign?"

"No," everyone at the table echoed.

Warren looked at Trey, "You have suggestions?"

"Will you listen to them?" Trey inquired. "I'm not going to bother if you're not serious about improving. I'll just shut your team down and transfer the Clan Smertae to another region."

Dawn nudged Warren, "You don't want that! It's not fair to the other Knights and lords under you."

"No, I don't. Dawn's right, it wouldn't be fair to the other guys on the team." Warren agreed. "Lochwood," he said judiciously, "I know I'm not the easiest person. But I do care about this game." He looked at the others at the table. "Maybe more than I should, more than is reasonable, because I let it become my everything. I don't want you shutting us down. It wouldn't be fair to the Smertae to force them to go to another arena."

"That's what I wanted to hear," Trey said. "I have suggestions on a few change ups. I'd like to see both sides put the weapons down for one or two tourneys and play the board game as it was intended to be played. We can go from there, and I will supervise." He looked at the food that had been served, "Let us continue this discussion as we enjoy this meal."

DURING THE MEAL THEY were entertained by a singer and by a comic. After dinner, when the tables were cleared, the orchestra above started to play dance music. Warren asked Dawn to dance, and Tim and Caitlyn also moved to the dancefloor. They looked a bit awkward with Caitlyn's arm in her sling.

Trey looked at Barbara, "May I have this dance?" he asked.

"No." Barbara said quietly.

Trey frowned, "Have I offended you?"

"No, Mr. Lochwood," she said shaking her head, "you've been wonderful company."

"Then what is it? Are you afraid of being accused of beguiling me?" his face softened, and he smiled again. "I'm mean I'm flattered..."

"I can't dance," she said in a rush. "I never learned how."

Trey went still, the smile vanished, and he blinked, "What?"

"I never learned how to dance," she whispered, hoping she'd not be overheard. She looked to the side, grateful that no one seemed to care about the conversation she was having with Trey Lochwood.

He leaned back, "What do you mean you never learned?" he asked in as quiet a voice as she'd used.

"The nuns at the convent schools I attended didn't think it was important for *me* to learn that part of the social graces." She muttered, giving into the anger that was always inside her. "Excuse me," she said, rising she move toward the lobby. A voice halted her in the lobby.

"Barra," Trey used her game name, "wait."

Her steps ceased, her back went ridged, and her head turned slightly. "Skald," she addressed him by his game title, making sure she said it correctly. "There is nothing more to say."

"Isn't there?" he challenged as he stepped closer. He extended his arm out, waiting for her to place her hand upon his cuffed band. She exhaled, and placed her hand where it was expected, and he strolled with her to an empty alcove. "I'm sorry, I didn't mean to upset you." He motioned for her to take a seat.

She looked up at him, "It's a foolish thing to get upset about, I know. It's prideful and foolish."

"No," he disagreed. "I'm sure it doesn't feel foolish at all." He motioned her to be seated. "From the moment I saw you," he explained. "I could tell you were different from everyone else." He took a seat opposite her, "You're a bit younger I think then the rest of your group," she nodded, "I thought so." He held out a hand to her. "What were you doing in a convent school? If you don't mind my asking."

Barbara thought about it, then made the choice, she was going to trust her instincts about this man. "I'm an orphan," she explained without emotions. "My parents passed when I was a small child, my guardian didn't want me around. I've been in a convent school, several actually since I was five."

"Five?" he repeated.

"Five," she nodded. "The sisters were to educate me, but not to indulge me. Or at least what I heard two of them saying when discussing me." She could feel her cheeks color, "I wasn't supposed to hear, but its rather hard to not hear what is being discussed right in front of you."

Trey looked pained, "That stinks."

"It does, but it is what it is," she agreed. "I spent day in and day out learning, reading, and because of it, I qualified for a scholarship. That's why I'm here." She looked down at the shoes that Caitlyn's mother had lent her. "Everything I've got, this dress, the makeup, even these shoes are part of the generosity I've been shown by Caitlyn O'Hara's family since I arrived here in Danbury. I wouldn't be here had she not taken pity on me and befriended me." She stood up, "I shouldn't be here." Her voice hardened. "I really don't belong here; the Sisters of No Hope saw to that. I'm an outcast."

Trey stood up and put his hands on her arms, "I doubt your friends, even Warren would agree with you."

"Warren is going to wake up and hate me for having humiliated him." Barbara said harshly. "And when that happens..."

SIGN OF THE RAVEN

"Barra," again he used her game name, almost as an endearment. "When I came that day to the tourney, I was ready to shut the branch of our franchise down, I was so filled with angry for what they had done to the game. Then I saw you." One hand moved to tilt her face up, "You instinctually went into action to protect Caitlyn. Your movements were poetry! Graceful, and deadly, and yet you showed more mercy than was being shown to you. You saved Warren from himself, I have a feeling that his girlfriend Dawn is letting him know just that." He smiled at her, "So, your life hasn't been all sunshine and light up until now. Those nuns didn't think you should learn how to socialize, and they were wrong. As for dancing, that's easy. I'll teach you if you'll let me." He offered. "Anyone who can wield a pike as you did, can dance."

"Why?" She pulled back slightly, "Why would you do such a thing?"

"First, because I like you," he admitted. "And secondly, I want you to dance with me."

She stared at him, was he kidding? No, his face wasn't mocking, nor was he being a tease. "You really think you can teach me to dance?"

"Maybe not the jiggling gyration that they like to do," he pointed to the ballroom they had exited. "But the kind of dancing that goes with our costumes, oh yes!" He raised a hand, "Listen, they are playing a folk song, this one is easy. Just do what I do." He held his hands out and began to talk her through the simple folk dance. "Face the same direction as me," he said as he held her hands, "Look at our reflection in that mirror there. It's a right step, left step, hop, hop. Tilt to the left, tilt to the right, hop, hop. Repeat." He applied gentle pressure to her hand as he directed her steps. "That's it... you've got it." He praised. "Not so hard, is it?"

"No," she said breathily, "that was fun."

"Let me show you a few more steps and we'll be ready to take to the floor." He promised.

"Thank you, Mr. Lochwood..."

He smiled, "I'd like you to call me Trey."

When he said she was ready they returned to the ballroom, he led her to the dance floor and led the next reel with her. After that, they danced every folk dance that came up.

"THIS WAS THE BEST BIRTHDAY I've ever had," Barbara said to Caitlyn when they all took a break from dancing. She sipped the sparkling cider that had been served.

"I didn't know today was your birthday," Caitlyn pouted. "You should have told me."

"The nuns never celebrated it, so I had no reason to," She took another sip of the cider. "But this one makes up for all the rest."

"Oh Barb," Dawn sat down and reach out a hand to the draped opening of her sleeve, "I had no idea you went in for tats."

"It's not," Barbara said, "It's a birthmark, or so I was told."

"It looks like the outline for a tat," Dawn teased. "That looks familiar."

Barbara nodded, "It resembles a kind of rune, doesn't it?"

Trey was leaning on her chair, "Let me see," he moved to inspect her arm. He watched as the others moved back to the dance floor. "That's not a birthmark, or at least not a natural one." He said softly when the others had gone. "This was done by an artist."

"The doctor said it wasn't ink," she said. "Someone wanted him to remove it, and he said he couldn't without taking the whole arm."

"It's not ink, it's a kind of brand made with pins in a special jig and a stain." He advised. "Only a few Celt families still do this." He looked closer, "From the color, I can say this was done when you were young. Maybe even when you were still a baby. But it wasn't finished."

"Finished?" she said.

He nodded, "As the brand ages, it is filled in with special dyes made from flower pastes to complete the stain."

Barbara looked at everyone dancing, then back at Trey, "Does it mean something?"

"It's two runes put together," Trey said. "I think it means you're a child of the house of the Raven."

She looked away, "Trey, promise not to say any more about this right now. I'll explain when I can."

"Barra," he turned her face back to him, "I'll do whatever you ask."

"Thank you." She said.

"Don't look so sad," he begged. "Come and dance with me again."

She stood up, "Are you really going to supervise our tourneys?"

"Does it worry you?" he asked.

Barbara looked over at Warren and Dawn dancing, "Some of the Anglo/Roman crowd might take offence," she warned. "The Celtic Norse will look at it as just another challenge."

"Warren and his crowd have turned this game upside down over the last eight years. I'm not blaming Warren for it all, but it's gotten out of hand under him and his crew." Trey led her to the dance floor, "If I'm there, they will all have to play by the rules."

"Perhaps some of them will even read the rules," Barbara quipped.

"Perhaps," he agreed. "And maybe, just maybe, the girls will get a chance to be more active!"

Chapter 4.

Four years later, Barbara was still spending most of her holidays and off times at the O'Hare house. The family had more, or less, adopted her. She and Caitlyn were working hard to finish five-year degrees in only four years which meant taking summer classes as well. Barbara was glad her scholarship covered costs of summer classes. An unexpected windfall had come her way when she'd been asked to tutor some of her classmates. She had opened a savings account as well as the checking account her allowance had provided and was paying for luxury items from this fund, over and beyond what her allowance paid for. She was establishing credit and learning how to manage her own funds. Things others took for granted, things other students had been taught by their families, she had to learn on her own. She had a plan, and it didn't include ever going back to the convent.

Tim had finished the three associate degrees he needed to satisfy his father and had gone into the engineering department of his father's construction company. Both girls missed him on campus and made the most of what time they could spend with him on his days off. They still made time for coffee and doughnuts, and of course the game.

Every weekend after Thanksgiving each year, they met with the others in their branch of the Conquest at the abandoned mall and practiced. Now, even the girls were swinging weapons, and everyone had taken up archery. The one-time rivalry had dissolved, and Warren had begun to mend fences with his classmates of all social statuses. Trey still came out to keep tabs on the progress of the gamers; or so he'd said.

When the annual Solstice Ball arrived, so did Trey. This year he showed up on campus the week after Thanksgiving, grinning. "Barra!" he called out and waved as he strutted across the campus toward her and Caitlyn. "So glad I ran into you! I thought I was going to have to hunt you down."

"Not a hard task for you," she teased. "What brings you to Danbury, Skald?"

SIGN OF THE RAVEN

"You," he said, then smiled at Caitlyn, "Hi, Caiti, how are you?"

"Fine Trey, how are you?"

"Working hard," he said, "could you give Barra and I a moment?"

Caitlyn nodded, "I'll see you in the lab, and this time, don't forget your book."

"You forgot a book?" Trey inquired. "How did that happen?"

"I left it in the park, I was running late." Barbara admitted. "It was just before Thanksgiving when we had that warm spell."

"Ah," he laughed. "I can see how that would make you forget things."

Barbara pulled her coat tighter, "Could use that warm snap right now."

"Come and sit with me," he pointed to an empty bench. "There's something I want to ask you."

"Okay," she agreed.

When they had taken their seats, he placed his arm over the top of the bench, "I wanted to ask you to be my date to the Solstice ball this year," he said.

"Date?"

"Date," he nodded, "not just my dinner partner, but an honest to goodness date." He smiled. "I know it's your birthday, and that you turn *twenty-one* and are all *legal*, and I don't have to worry about being accused of leading a minor down the road to hell."

"Trey," she groaned. "You've such a way with words."

He laughed, "Don't I?" He placed the hand that had been resting on the bench on her shoulder. "You're not going with anyone else, are you?"

"No," she admitted. "But you know that I'm ... awkward."

"Not with me, you're not." He leaned closer. "Are you?"

"Not usually," she agreed. "I don't know why."

"Because I understand you," he said. "You and I come from the same kind of people."

"Do we?"

"Yes."

Barbara looked away, "You at least know your people, I don't."

"I've offered countless times to help you look for answers," he reminded her. "Every time, you've rejected my offer."

"It's not that I didn't appreciate the offer," she told him. "Until I'm legal age, I don't want to bring attention to myself." She looked back at him. "My guardian will have no more say over me the day I turn twenty-one. I intend to look for answers to my questions then, and only then."

"What are you afraid of?" he questioned.

"Trey, I don't even know the name of my guardian, I know nothing about her, except that she was extremely angry when she learned she couldn't put me in the convent for good. She was furious that I have rights and a choice in this and other matters. And the only reason I know, is the new Bishop didn't like the wall of secrecy that was surrounding me." She took a deep breath, "I have a feeling that mark on my arm, the one you said was a family brand, has a lot to do with that."

"Okay," he said. "But I want to help when you're ready to start hunting down the truth."

She reached up for his hand, "You have been a help, more than I could have asked for," she assured him. "Teaching me to dance and being so wonderful about the Danbury branch of the game." She sighed, "Giving them a chance has meant all the difference in how they are playing now."

"I want to help *you*, Barra." He took a deep breath, "In case it's escaped you, I've developed a very deep fondness for you. I'd like to take it further along."

"Date?" she said uncertainly.

"Date," his voice dropped and became throaty. He leaned in closer, until his forehead touched hers. "How are we ever going to fall in love and get married if you won't even date me?"

"Trey!" she admonished. "Don't talk nonsense."

"Seriously, sweetheart," he droned on, "I have been your dinner partner for three years, in case you've not noticed. I show up at your tourneys but have kept my distance so that neither of us would have legal troubles, but you're turning twenty-one! I can't be accused of leading a minor down the wrong path any longer. I know I'm older than you, but I don't think seven years is that much of a gap. This year, I don't want to be just your dinner partner, I want to be your *date*!"

"Date?" she repeated.

He nodded against her head, "I want to pick you up at your door, in my car, escort you to the dinner and spend the evening basking in your attention."

"You're demented." She muttered.

"Be that as it may," he teased back, "I want to spend the evening with *you* on my arm and then get a good old-fashioned good night kiss at your door. The first of many, I do hope."

"I'll be staying at Caitlyn's," she interrupted his campaign. "Tim usually takes us both in..."

"Tim and Caitlyn are dating," he reminded her. "Warren and Dawn are a dating couple. You don't have to ride in with them, you can date. There's no law against it."

"Trey," she sighed, "You know I'm socially awkward. The nuns didn't prepare me for the world."

"Time to combat that," he said, not put off. "Besides, I've never noticed you having one single awkward moment with me."

"You're not going to drop this, are you?"

He shook his head, "No, I'm not, I am determined."

"I don't date," she reminded him.

"It's time you started," he countered, "and I'm the man you are going to date."

"You're crazy," she said, but smiled despite herself.

"About you," he admitted. "Have been totally smitten since the moment our eyes met."

"Trey," she moaned.

"Barra," he moaned back. "Give it a try, you might find you like it."

She pulled away from him, "I don't know."

"Would it help," he pulled two tickets out of his pocket, "if I said I already bought the tickets?" he wiggled them at her.

"I don't believe you!"

"Believe it!" he said. "Now, be a good girl, and say yes."

"On one condition," she said.

"No conditions," he argued.

"One," she repeated. "No more talk of falling in love and futures. Not just yet." Barbara felt as if a goose had walked on her grave, "I don't want to jinx what is happening."

Rolling his eyes, he shrugged, "Fine, have it your way," he said. "We date and worry about the rest later."

"Trey, I'm serious, until I find out about my past, I don't want to get knee deep in a relationship." She told him.

"Too late, we are already in a relationship," he quipped. "I was serious about wanting to help track your past down," he reminded her. "I have resources you don't have." He tucked the tickets back into his coat. "I promised to wait until you turned twenty-one, on Solstice that wait is over, for both of us. We can being the search for the truth together."

She looked at him, "You've waited four years?" She shook her head, "You don't expect me to believe you didn't date during that time, do you?"

"Barra," he laughed, "you have more sense than that. Of course, I dated, just not seriously. I took girls out but have been a perfect gentleman since I met you." He shrugged, "No one said you couldn't date, did they?"

"The nuns did," she looked away, "So many things have been crammed into my head by the nuns... Starting with me being the demon spawn."

"Did they really tell you not to date?" he asked.

"There was a tradition," she whispered, "a cotillion, just before high school graduation from the school." He nodded, "I was not allowed to attend. My guardian refused to pay for the gown and said no one in his right mind would escort me." She fought the tears. "Mother Clare wasn't happy about telling me and had the decency to keep it private. Mother Clare was far more kind then Mother Angelica had been. But on the day of the ball, I... had to watch as my classmates descended the staircase into the lobby and were escorted into the hall. I wasn't even allowed to be part of the class picture, because I didn't have a ballgown to descend the stair in."

"Your guardian might have thought that isolating you would prevent you from joining the world, as she intended you to take convent vows," he said firmly. "But you are stronger than they knew." He tipped her face upward, "Barra, I am not going to allow you to be isolated any longer."

"Trey, why do you care? I'm not pretty, I'm not popular, I'm no one and nothing."

"You're beautiful, majestic and more powerful than you know," he assured her. "And you are perfect for me." He brushed her tears away, "Date?" he whispered.

"Date." She nodded.

THE NIGHT BEFORE THE ball, Caitlyn and Tim drove Barbara over to Caitlyn's parent's house. Just as they had in the past few years. Mrs. O'Hara greeted the trio with warm mugs of mulled cider. When Tim left, Mrs. O'Hara sat down with the girls, "Did you bring everything?" she asked Barbara.

"No, just the essentials," she said. "I'm still not sure about this."

"You're welcome here," Mrs. O'Hara said firmly. "We've told you over and over."

"I know," Barbara nodded, "But in the back of my mind.... There's danger, and I don't want it to touch this family."

Caitlyn shrugged, "If she feels better staying in the dorm, I don't think we can change her mind, mom."

"You are the closest thing I have to a family," Barbara said. "I'm going to protect you all." Shaking her head, she went on. "I don't know anything about who I am, or why my guardian told the nuns I was the devil's spawn. Or why this last guardian tried to railroad me into taking the veil! No, I'm not willing to take chances with you. You are more family to me than I've ever had." She took a deep breath, "I won't chance your safety. I don't know what the guardian is going to pull now that I'm turning legal age."

"I hate the idea of you staying in that dorm," Mrs. O'Hara murmured. "It's so isolated."

"My entire existence since I was five is one of isolation," Barbara said softly. "Unraveling that is going to take time and will have to start in secret. I don't want them, the guardian and the others to figure out I'm on to them."

"Everything changes after tomorrow," Mrs. O'Hara warned. "You will no longer be under any obligation to this guardian who didn't even have the decency to meet you."

"That's true," Barbara agreed, "however, I have to move carefully. My scholarship is intact, and I want it to remain so. But I'm not going to have the allowance I had during the past few years. I have to move carefully, not overspend or get ahead of myself."

"With the money you've put into that savings account, you should have enough to see you through the rest of the school year," Caitlyn said softly. "You've already put money aside for the fees for graduation."

"This is one graduation I intend to make it too." Barbara vowed.

SIGN OF THE RAVEN

Caitlyn sipped her cider, "I can't believe they made you sit and watch while your classmates got their diplomas." Her bitterness sounded like it reflected the bitterness that Barbara felt. "Handing you yours after the ceremony, out of sight and out of mind."

"It's in the past," Barbara said. "What the Nuns did, what my guardians did. From here on out, it's what I do that counts."

"Dating Trey Lochwood is a good start," Caitlyn raised her mug in salute.

"Dating who?" Mrs. O'Hara asked. She smiled at Barbara, "Since when?"

"He asked her to be his *date* to the ball, not just his dinner partner." Caitlyn said. "He's picking her up and everything!"

Mrs. O'Hara looked over at Barbara, who shrugged, "He was persistent."

"Speaking of persistent," Mrs. O'Hara looked at the clock, "your brother's plane should have landed. Dad is picking him up."

"At long last I get to speak to the illusive Jason in person," Barbara teased.

AN HOUR LATER, JASON came in the back door and went straight to his mother's open arms. Barbara understood the feeling they conveyed. If not in person, through this family. She watched as the mother welcomed back her warrior son, and he surrendered to her.

Mr. O'Hara placed an arm over his daughter, and the other over Barbara. "Worth seeing." He said.

Barbara leaned in at the same time Caitlyn did. "So worth it." She agreed.

Jason looked over at his sister, "Where's my welcome?" he challenged. Answered by a blur of Caitlyn moving his way and wrapping her arms about him.

He looked at Barbara whom he'd only spoken to on the skype. "Okay, adopted sis, come and hug me." Barbara moved toward him slower than Caitlyn had, but her welcoming hug was just as genuine. The arms about her were genuine as well. "I'm so happy to meet my new sister at last!"

Dinner with the long gong son back was even more lively than before. Caitlyn and Molly got Jason caught up on what was going on in town and who had run off with whom. Barbara enjoyed listening to the banter between bother and sisters. When the meal was over the subject turned to the Solstice Ball.

"I remember those," Jason reminisced, "the gaming crowd wasn't quiet as large as it is now, and most of the attendees were in tuxes and gowns back then."

"They still are," Caitlyn said, "in fact, they petitioned to make the gamers comport."

"Figures," Jason murmured. "I'm surprised the Beckett kid is in the game and not on the other side." He tilted his nose up with one finger, "Old money will out."

"He's one of our best gaming members." Barbara said, surprised she was feeling supportive of Warren. "He's done a lot to make the game more interesting in the last four years."

"He switched sides," Caitlyn told her brother.

"He did what?" Jason reacted with understandable awe.

"He became a member of Barbara's household in the Celts and brought most of his house with him." Caitlyn nodded.

"You're head of your own house?" Jason asked.

"It didn't start that way, but when I took his castle..."

"Wait," he held up his hand, "you took his castle?"

"It's a long story," Barbara looked at Caitlyn, "I thought you told him."

"That Warren fractured my arm?" she asked.

"He what?" Jason stood up.

"Sit down," Mr. O'Hara ordered. "Be quiet and listen, Barb, you tell him."

"Warren thought he could impress the visiting officials by assaulting our stand. In the process, he got a bit overzealous and hit Caitlyn with his rattan sword with more force than he meant to. I grabbed a pike and knocked him on his ass and killed his persona." Barbara explained, "He called foul. The officials said it was a good kill and since Tim had gifted me with a membership it held. I don't know if they would have kept it had it not been for that, and the fact that Warren by attacking us drew us in the game. When the official said the kill stood, I turned around and led a shield maiden assault on his fortress while his knights were on the battlefield, and took all his house as my banner-members."

"She almost single handedly took the castle," Caitlyn nodded, "with the battle cry, 'How many of them can we make die'?"

"Oh, I wish I'd seen that," Jason claimed.

"We have it on disk," Mr. O'Hara said. "I'll play it for you later."

Jason nodded a little too eagerly.

"The next year, when Warren was eligible to play again, he shifted his side and became my first steward." Barbara shrugged. "Dawn came with him and so did almost all the girls who had been in his castle. They said they would rather be my banner maidens than be with their boyfriends. They were sick of being dressed up like wilting lilies. As my banner maidens they were allowed to dress much more like real people, not window dressing."

Jason laughed, "That must have thrilled his father."

"Not so much," Caitlyn interjected. "Barbara had taken his helm and shield and sword and cloak as trophies that first day. The old man wanted to sue her to get them back and wanted her barred from the game."

"Warren refused to take part in a suit," Barbara said.

"What changed?" Jason asked. "When I left here, he was a miserable spoiled brat." Jason shrugged, "Not much different than his older brothers."

"Barbara knocked him on his ass twice and threated to hand him his balls." Caitlyn said.

"He took her at her word," Mr. O'Hara nodded. "Took a good look at himself when she called him a bully at the Solstice Ball in front of Trey Lochwood."

"Nearly cost him Dawn." Caitlyn agreed.

"Really?" Jason looked at Barbara. "And he's been loyal to you?"

"Extremely," Barbara said. "Not that I trusted it for the first year, but last year and this, he's been fantastic."

"He even joined the history discussion group," Caitlyn said. "It went far beyond the let's play with swords stuff, and he got Tim to be more serious about the history. Then he hired Barbara to tutor him so he could pass his exams and get his degree!"

"And he and Dawn are getting married in the spring," Barbara added. "He finished his degree with this last term, and she gets her teaching degree for art this spring." Barbara bragged, "Her art exhibit was paintings and photos she took while being in the stand at tourney!"

"Things really have changed while I was gone," Jason said. "I'm not surprised but I am amazed at how much and how fast."

"Warren's father isn't happy that Warren still wants to be part of the Conquest game." Caitlyn said. "I think he's planning on making it harder for him to participate."

"We can worry about that after the ball," Barbara warned. "I'm looking forward to showing off my new gown."

"It is stunning," Caitlyn said. "Shows off her arm brand."

"Arm brand?" Jason turned to Barbara. "You've got an arm brand?" He teased his sister, "You're running with a fast crowd, tats and all."

SIGN OF THE RAVEN

"I've had it since I was little," she nodded. "I don't know much about it. Trey says that only some old families still practices this type. He said that he thinks it means belonging to the Raven."

Jason frowned, "Could I see this brand?"

"Sure," she said without being self-conscious, and rolled up her sleeve. "It's pretty faded," she explained. "Whoever did it wasn't around to finish the job. My parents died when I was little."

Jason traced the outline with his finger, and shook his head, "Trey's translation is a little off. It's not belonging to the Raven; it says the bearer is the Raven."

"What does that mean?" Barbara asked.

"I'd have to look into the Celt houses who use this." Jason said. "But it's sort of a mixed rune, Celtic and Norse."

"How do you know how to read this?" Caitlyn challenged. "You didn't read runes when you left here."

"My buddy has one," Jason said. "He liked showing it off and explaining the signs. A bunch of us were thinking of getting the rune tats." He saw his mother flinch and said. "We didn't because we didn't like the guy in the little town near our station who did them. It didn't look clean."

"Thank heaven." His mother said.

Barbara looked at her arm, "Trey says that in Scotland they still do this with the old pins and irons and plant dyes."

"He's right about that." Jason nodded, "Just not his translation."

"Raven was a sign of death," Caitlyn said. "Wasn't it?"

"Not always," Jason said. "It depends on which house did this."

Barbara pondered how it was that Jason got the meaning wrong.

Jason traced it again, "You know, we could do a henna wash on this so it shows how it should look."

"We could?" Barbara looked at her arm, "In time for the Ball?"

BOTH TREY AND TIM PULLED into the drive at the same time, Caitlyn frowned. "I don't see why he can't just meet you at the venue."

"He argued that wouldn't be a date," Barbara stated. "He says that you and Tim date without me, and we can date without you."

"It's not like I'm watching over the two of you," Caitlyn complained. "I've got better things to do."

"Trey has this idea in his head that we are going to be a couple." Barbara said, trying to sooth her friend. "Long term."

"Are you?"

Barbara was putting her cloak on, "I don't know," she answered. "I've got some questions that need answers before I commit to anyone."

"Mind if I ask what?" Caitlyn too was putting on a cloak.

"This is between me and Trey," Barbara told her. "Once I have my answers, then I'll tell you." She promised.

Caitlyn shrugged. "Okay, if that's how you want it."

Barbara placed a hand on her friend's arm, "That's how it has to be, this time. I'm trying to keep you and your family safe from whatever fallout that's coming my way."

The doorbell rang, and Caitlyn answered, both young men stepped in. Tim whistled low and then growled. Caitlyn giggled.

Trey moved to stand opposite Barbara. "Barra," he bowed to her.

"Trygve," she answered softly, and dropped into a gentle curtsey.

"You look wonderful," he said handing her a wrist corsage. He turned to Caitlyn's parents. "Mr. O'Hara, Mrs. O'Hara." He gave them a curt bow. "Nice to see you."

"Lochwood," Mr. O'Hara was equally curt, and Barbara wondered if there were bad vibes there.

"You all look so wonderful," Mrs. O'Hara said much warmer a greeting than her husband's.

Jason leaned on the frame of the arch to the dining room. "Tim, do I have to tell you what happens if you don't bring my sister back in good order?"

SIGN OF THE RAVEN

"When did you get home?" Tim got defensive. He looked at Caitlyn, "You didn't tell me he was back."

"I didn't think I had to," she was glaring at her brother.

"I mean it, Tim," Jason warned.

"Jason!" his mother snapped.

Trey looked at Jason, "Would you like to extend that threat to me as well?"

"Yes," Jason nodded, "I happen to like our orphan," he said sassily. "And I want her returned just as we loan her out."

"I'm not on loan," Barbara said.

"Don't bet on it," Jason warned her. "You're our orphan, and don't you forget it."

"I promise to return her intact," Trey teased back, silencing Barbara's protest.

"Good," Jason sipped his coffee. "Now, go, get out of my sight the lot of you and have fun."

"Just not too much," Trey finished for him. "Nice to see you again, Jason."

"Same here, Lochwood." He finished his coffee and left the room.

Trey nodded to the O'Hara parents and held his arm out to Barbara, "Your chariot awaits you," he said softly. Barbara wasn't sure she still wanted to go, she hesitated. Trey seeing her hesitance whispered, "You'll have to forgive Jason and I our barbs back and forth," he explained placing her hand in the crook of his arm, "He and I go way back, and were sparing partners in several sports. We were the Tim and Warren of our day."

"I'm no one's orphan," she complained, casting a disparaging glance over her shoulder to where Jason had been standing. "And I am not on loan."

Trey smiled at her, "Of course not," he agreed. "You'll have to get use to Jason's way of talking about things."

"He didn't mean to be rude," Caitlyn said from behind Barbara. "I don't know what comes over him sometimes."

"He's a big brother," Tim grumbled.

"He's not mine," Barbara complained.

"Don't tell him," Trey advised. "He's already accepted you into the O'Hara clan, be thankful. It's a fine family to be associated with."

They separated at the cars, Tim ushered Caitlyn into his, and Trey held the passenger door on his sedan open for Barbara. "We're lucky the snow is holding off," Trey said as he pulled out of the drive. "The roads are dry, and we shouldn't have any trouble getting there. There have been balls that were called off because of winter storms." He explained.

Barbara became lost in thoughts as they drove. When he pulled into the lot, she could contain her thoughts no more. She placed her hand on his as he switched off the engine. "I need to know something," she said. "If you give me the wrong answer, this date is over." She announced.

Trey looked at her, "Barra," he was shocked.

"I need to know if you are intentionally misleading me," she said. "Jason said you misread the brand on my arm." She accused. "He says it reads This is the Raven, not She belongs to the Raven."

Trey raised a brow, and then nodded, he reached into the back seat. When his arm came back over, he placed a wrapped package on Barbara's lap. "I was going to give this to you later, but now is better."

She eyed the package with suspicion. "What is this?"

"It's a present," he said. "Open it."

"A present?"

"For your birthday," he nodded.

"I don't get presents," she whispered, "Only recently have I gotten any, and they have been from Caitlyn." She corrected. She lifted the lid and looked inside. The top page was a copy of her brand, and she looked at him, "What is this?"

SIGN OF THE RAVEN

"Four years ago," Trey explained softly, "after I saw that brand, I had a feeling that I might have misread it. So, I went to a friend of my father who is an authority on the subject and asked a few questions."

"You did?" She questioned, "you didn't say anything."

He nodded, "I roughly drew out what is on your arm and my father's friend translated it much better. He also gave me the leads on who uses the brand of the Raven." He lifted the first page and a list of names was on the second page. "I told you, I have resources."

Barbara stared at the names, and the page with her brand. "I don't know what to say."

"Barra," his voice went deep. "I don't think your last name is Gowan."

She looked up at him, "You don't?"

Shaking his head, he went on, "I think that was your mother's name. Her maiden name, and your Grandmother's name."

"And the mystery deepens," she said dejectedly.

"I told you, I want to help." Trey said. "I am not trying to distract or mislead you. I didn't give this to you before, because you told me on that first Solace Ball that you wanted to wait until you were of legal age."

"I'm sorry for accusing you," she whispered.

"You don't trust many people," he observed. "Up until now, I'd say you had good reason not to."

"You've no idea." She sighed.

"I'm on your side," he promised. "I want us to get closer."

"Why?" she asked, "I'm awkward, I've been held back..."

"I don't care about any of that," he explained. "From the moment our eyes met, there was a spark. I want to pursue it." With a gentle movement, he brushed aside the hair that had fallen on her face. "Give me a chance."

She nodded, "Alright Trey," she agreed. "This," she placed her hand over the pages in her lap, "this means the world to me. That you did this." She looked up at him, "I've put it off, fearing that someone would stop me, or that my guardian would get word..."

"I didn't mention you," he promised. "I was exploring that brand, not the girl wearing it."

"Thank you." She leaned forward, throwing caution to the wind, and kissed him. She pulled back, feeling embarrassed. "I'm sorry... I don't..."

"Don't be sorry," he said with a smile. "Was that the first time you've kissed someone?" when she nodded, he said. "I'm honored it was me." He placed his head against hers, "There's no need to rush, we've time to let this develop."

She took a deep breath, "I don't know what the future holds," she warned, "or what the people who did this to me are capable of."

"We'll face it, one day at a time, together." He promised. "I am not going to let you face this alone." His hand now rested on her shoulder, giving support without making her feel overwhelmed. "Whatever resources I have are yours for the asking."

"Thank you."

He pulled back, "Ready to face them in there," he pointed to the banquet hall.

She nodded and covered the box again. "I think we should leave this here. Let's keep this between us, for now."

"If you like," he answered.

She looked over at the banquet hall, "I haven't told most of them what I'm doing. Caitlyn and Tim know, but not the rest."

"I'm glad you told me, and that I could start you off on a path to look for your past." Trey said. He exited his side of the car and came around to hers. "This is your journey; you don't have to justify it to anyone." He assured her. Once more he offered her his arm, this time she placed her hand in the crook without any hesitation, "What lies ahead, you don't have to face alone. Not anymore."

"I don't want to endanger anyone else's future." She argued softly. "My future is mote."

"Not from where I stand," he countered.

"You are prejudice," she teased.

"Yes," he agreed as they strolled to the door. "I am."

THEY MOVED TO THEIR table after leaving their cloaks with the coatroom girl. Trey nodded, acknowledged the greeting they were receiving. When they reached the table, the others were already there.

"I was getting worried," Caitlyn said. "I thought something had gone wrong." She looked over at Trey.

"No," Barbara said. "Everything is fine."

Trey smiled, "Caiti," he said with humor. "Don't you trust me?"

"No," She said.

"I'm wounded," The teased.

"Easy Trey," Tim warned. "She's very protective of Barb there."

"Barra and I have an understanding," Trey said. "Don't we?" He looked at Barbara.

"We do," she agreed.

Warren leaned on the table, "Really?" He seemed interested. "And what would that be?"

"We are dating," Barbara said, as if that would end the discussion.

"Is that fair?" Warren challenged.

"What do you care, you are part of her house now," Trey teased.

"True, but..." Warren shrugged.

Barbara frowned at Warren, "I don't tell you who to date, do I?"

Warren held up his hands in surrender, "You know me, Barb, I have to stir the pot."

"Well knock it off," she ordered. "Trey and I are just getting to know each other."

"I haven't seen you date anyone before," Warren commented. "In fact, I don't know if anyone has asked."

"She said, knock it off," Dawn reminded him, before she changed the subject. "Are you taking the final course in the history of the middle ages?" she asked Barbara.

"I'm planning on being a history major," Barbara answered. "I'd like to teach the subject."

"Teaching," Warren shuddered.

"Someone has to," Tim shrugged.

"I think Barb will be a great teacher," Dawn said defensively. "She loves the subject; she'll make it come to life."

"But it's so cut and dry, not like the game." Warren argued. "Surely you don't want to have to face a classroom of knothead kids like me." Trey laughed, and so did Barbara. Warren paused and laughed too. "I just hate the idea of you not having fun."

"But History is fun for me," she said. "If I can get one person to understand why it's important, and that you need subjects like history, I would feel like I made a difference." She pointed at Tim, "I got him through the class."

"Actually," Tim said, "it did make playing Conquest more fun."

WHEN THE DINNER AND dance ended, everyone parted on good terms. Tim and Caitlyn left ahead of Trey and Barbara who were saying good night to a lot of the attendees. When they got to his car, he opened the door.

"That was fun," he said.

"I had no idea that Warren had such resentment against teachers." Barbara said entering his vehicle.

Trey came around to the driver's side, "One would think, having a family who is in history, he'd be more interested."

"I thought being so involved in the game, he'd be more interested." Trey pulled onto the highway but turned off on to another road. "Where are we going?" She asked. "This isn't the way back to the O'Hara place."

"I know," he said. "There's something out here in the valley I want you to see."

"Okay," she said.

He drove past the Revolutionary war memorial, and then turned on a road to where an apple orchard was. "This is the old Morgan place, isn't it?" she asked.

"It was the Morgan place," he nodded. And he pulled across a bridge, "It's the Lochwood place now." He pulled up and turned off the engine. There was scaffolding and construction equipment, and yellow caution tape. He turned to look at her, "What do you think?"

She looked at the once charming old house, "What are you doing?"

"Fixing the roof, expanding out back and upgrading the house." He said, motioning up to the roofline and beyond. "In the spring, I'm having the orchard buildings upgraded and expanded." He opened the glovebox and pulled out some snap shots, "The house was getting rundown; however, I think it's worth saving. Do you know the history of this place?" She nodded, "Morgan's kids didn't want any part of the business, and rather than see this all become condos and little ticky tacky houses, I bought it. The house is pretty much what sold me."

"What do you know about orchards?" She challenged.

"Not enough," he admitted, "however, I am taking a course, and I've hired the foreman that Morgan had. So, we'll be on track for next year's crop and for the cider press come next fall."

"What possessed you to do this?" she asked.

"My father once said that land is a good thing," Trey said, "it's tangible; growing apples is a good thing. I have plans to expand the orchard, maybe add a few other fruits." He pointed to an open field.

"Two years ago, Morgan planted strawberries and blackberries. I'm going to make sure his plans go on."

"I had no idea you were so..."

"Well, I am," he teased. "That house was in the Morgan family for nearly two hundred years. It started as a little cottage and got added on to with each generation. It's a good house, it has good bones."

"Good bones?" She looked at the scaffolding, "I admit, I thought it was charming when we came out here in the fall."

"You and Caiti came out here?" Trey asked.

"A lot of Danbury comes out here for apples," she said. "Sort of a tradition kind of thing, Caitlyn said."

"Then it makes sense to save it, and keep it going." Trey said. "Think of how awful it would have been if this had been turned into another Markham Place."

The idea of cramped townhouses, and cookie cutter houses didn't set well. "They would have ruined the place." She agreed. "What about the pond?" she asked, "Caitlyn and I came here to skate last year, will we still be able to?"

"I've had the back entrance reopened, so it has its own drive and the pond will have a warming hut and benches." Trey nodded. "I used to come here to skate as a boy too, like a good many other locals." He told her. "I love this place."

"Enough to make it your home?"

"Mine, and yours if you're willing someday." He mused. "It would be a great place to have kids." He added.

"We just started dating, you've got us having kids?" She asked with a bit of ice. "Don't you think we should see how this dating goes?"

"We'll be fine," he said. "I know in my heart that you and I are right for one another."

"Trey," she moaned, "I don't even know what is going to happen to me in the next weeks. I expect a visit from my guardian's lawyer to try and shatter my world and my life." She shook her head, "I don't have time to plan a future."

"Nonsense." He said and pulled a little jewelry box out of the glovebox. He handed it to her.

Barbara stared at it, "I agreed to a date," she warned him. "Not an engagement."

"Open it," he urged.

Reluctantly she opened the box, but it wasn't a ring. On the inner bed lay a pendant, a Thor's Hammer with Celtic knots. "Oh, Trey." She gasped. "It looks like the one you wear."

"I agree, it's much too early for an engagement ring," he said lightly. "Although not too early for something to tell everyone that you're my girl." He lifted it and the chain out of the box. "Let me put it on you." Once it was secured to her neck he smiled, bent forward, and kissed her cheek, "Happy Birthday, Barra."

"Thank you, Trey." She placed her fingers to his face. "It's lovely."

"You're lovely, that pales in comparison."

She felt her checks flush, "No, I'm not. I can see my reflection in the mirror."

Trey pulled her closer, "You look with eyes, but not with heart," he cautioned. "I see the inner you, the woman of strength that even the nuns couldn't break." He sighed. "I see the woman who I want at my side as I journey through life, my own Shield Maiden. I see the Raven."

"Trey," she snuggled in, closer, feeling at ease with him. "I'm so used to having been called the devil's spawn, I have begun to believe it."

"You are no demon," he said. "But I doubt either of us would be called angels or saints."

"You don't know what you're taking on, Skald," she warned.

"I love a good mystery, Barra. Think of the fun we'll have unraveling it."

She looked up at him, "You think this is going to be fun?"

"Don't you?" he challenged. "I noticed you had a henna wash put on the brand. Now you are proclaiming to the world who and what you are."

"I'm afraid of what's going to happen," she whispered. "You don't understand, my guardian tried to force me to take the veil."

"What a waste that would be." Trey said.

"If the Bishop hadn't stepped in," she paused, and looked off into the distance. "You don't know the kind of people we're dealing with." She said.

"But it's we now," he assured her, "not just you."

Her hand closed about the pendant, "Alright, Trey." She said. "It's us. You and me against the world if need be."

"We'd better get you home," he suggested. "Jason is most likely pacing the floor."

She nodded.

He tipped her face upward and lowered his lips to hers, then when the kiss ended, he whispered. "My girl." She nodded again.

A short time later Trey pulled his car into the O'Hara drive. As predicted, Jason was pacing the porch. Trey parked came around the car and helped Barbara out. He held her elbow, lightly, as he escorted her to the porch. "Did we keep you up, Jason?" he teased.

"You're late," Jason looked at the watch on his wrist, "Tim got Caitlyn here half an hour ago."

"We stopped at the Morgan place," Trey said. "I wanted to show Barra the work we're doing."

"The Morgan place, you mean Morgan Orchards?" Jason asked

Trey nodded, "I bought it, and I'm having the house renovated." He stepped up to the porch with Barbara. "I wanted to show it to Barra."

"Why would *Barb* be interested?" Jason challenged putting emphasis on her English translation of her name.

"Because she's my *girl*," Trey said, turning to Barbara and kissing her lightly. "I'll call you in the morning, we'll make plans for Christmas."

He promised. "Maybe you and Caiti and Tim can come out for skating." He looked at Jason, "You're invited too."

"Ah huh," Jason said, unimpressed.

"Good night, Trey." Barbara turned him toward the car.

"What do you see in him?" Jason asked as they went into the house.

"He's good for me," Barbara assured the overprotective elder brother of her friend. "He's been very nice to me ever since we met." She added, "He didn't laugh when I told him I couldn't dance."

"What did he do?" Jason ask pausing at the stair.

Barbara smiled, "He taught me how to do several country and folk-dance steps."

"There's hope yet," Jason assured her. "Good night, orphan."

"Good night, warrior." She teased back. Jason paused, gave her words consideration, then nodded and went upstairs.

CHAPTER 5.

Four days later, on Christmas eve afternoon, the two couples were on the frozen pond. Trey provided hot chocolate in a thermos. The warming hut had been set up but by four he had sent the employees home for the holiday.

"So, you're really going to run the orchard?" Tim asked.

"I plan to." Trey nodded in agreement with the question. "My father said I was slowly dying in the office job I had taken. He said the only time I looked happy was when I was off to play the Conquest." He shrugged, "That's only a part time business, not a full-time job. This, this is a vocation; and that's far better than just a job. It's a way of life." He looked about at the bucolic scene. "And what a view; I'm going to love living out here."

"My dad said this orchard should have been a landmark," Caitlyn interjected into the conversation.

"I agree," Trey said firmly. "Everyone in the three towns nearest here, came here. For apples, for cider and for skating, some for picnics. Morgan's son lives on the west coast, he really doesn't care about the orchard, he never did. He couldn't get away from her quick enough. He was furious his father sold to me, and not to one of the land speculators. He said to the old man, he felt cheated out of the money they could have made." He shook his head in discuss. "Imagine telling your father that everything he'd worked for all his life meant nothing. That two hundred years of family history meant nothing, that the money meant more."

Tim sipped his hot chocolate. "Morgan's son said that?"

Trey nodded, "He called his father's lawyer to try and stop the sale to me from going through."

"I don't know these people," Barbara said. "I take it there's history here?"

Caitlyn explained, "This orchard is one of the last ones in the area. Most of the land here is so valuable, the farmers and the orchard owners have sold off. We used to be dairy country here."

"What happened?"

Trey frowned, "It's like Caitlyn said," he murmured. "The land got too valuable, the owners were talked into selling off. That began the little enclaves of ticky-tacky houses and condos. Used to be there were farmer markets out here, and dairy farms where you could buy fresh cheese and butter, and cream and eggs. The real stuff, not the stuff they sell as cream today in the grocery stores." He looked about the pond with a wistful expression. "I wanted to save this place and keep it like it is. I've started the legal work to get it registered as a historical site, and later we'll work on landmark status."

Barbara looked about too, "It is peaceful and magical." She agreed. "It feels special."

"I've got big plans for the place," Trey said. "Modernizing without sacrificing the charm!" He stood up, "There used to be a building here, and I'm going to have it rebuilt. A permanent warming station for winter, and a place to have picnics in the summer, maybe even a few wooden picnic tables. The haybarn that's at the back, I'm going to have renovated to use for weddings and parties. The cider press hasn't been used in the last five or six years, I'm going to have it fixed and ready to press next fall."

"Sounds expensive," Caitlyn warned.

"It will be, but I believe in this place." Trey announced. "I've asked old man Morgan if I can keep the name, Morgan's Orchards and he's agreed."

Caitlyn was still concerned. "It's just such a shame that he had to leave."

"He didn't leave," Trey said, "He's in the cottage behind the big house. I know how hard it was for him, selling off. I saw how much he loves the place. I plan on asking his advice every chance I get, keeping him involved. He's better off in the cottage, and he's still on the place and for as long as he can get around, he's free to roam where he wants."

"You kept him here?" Caitlyn sounded as if she didn't believe him.

"It's his home," Trey said. "Everyone who works here knows him, respects him and listens to what he says." He shrugged. "There's a lot I can learn from him."

Barbara listened, and then asked. "None of his children wanted to save the place? They would have let it be divvied?"

Tim nodded, "Places like this are divvied all the time, Barb."

"But you all just said how important this place was to you while you were growing up," she shook her head. "Wasn't it home to his children?"

"They have their own families now, and not one of them live out in the country." Trey sighed. "Like I said, his oldest son is out on the west coast, and has no intentions of ever coming back. His two daughters live in New York, in the city. His youngest son, I heard was a career

Army officer. He was the only one who seemed concerned about what was going to happen to his father."

"You mean the others... didn't care?" this conversation was upsetting to Barbara on so many levels. Not having grown up in a family, she couldn't imagine anyone being so callous.

"The daughters wanted the old man to live in a retirement center in the city. AS if that would make him happy." Trey explained. "Son number one didn't even ask. Youngest son was the one who was happy when I explained about the old cottage. Seems their grandmother lived in the cottage when they were kids, so I'm keeping a family tradition going."

Barbara was still frowning. "It doesn't seem right, them not caring."

"What they wanted wouldn't have been good for him. This way, he's surrounded by what he knows, he's safe and I intend to make sure he has a visiting nurse." Trey assured her. "I like the idea of him being here, and me being able to learn from him, and get his input on my ideas. He loved the idea of the wedding barn!"

Caitlyn softened, "Seems you saved more than just the orchard."

Tim pointed upward, "Looks like we might get another dusting of snow. A white Christmas for sure."

"Looks like a postcard out here," Barbara observed.

"I'm thinking of using part of that hill over there to grow Christmas trees, a cut your own farm." Trey told them. "Old man Morgan said he toyed with the idea, he even started planting fast growing evergreens. When his legs started giving him problems though he thought he should just stick to the orchard. The last five years, he ran the office, and didn't get out to the appletrees except in a golf cart."

"Do his daughters come out for the holidays?" Barbara inquired.

"Betty will this year," Trey said. "That's his youngest daughter, and she'll bring his teenaged grandkids."

"How big is that cottage?" Caitlyn teased.

"Big enough," Trey laughed. "His housekeeper opted to continue keeping house at the cottage. She looks after him as if he were family." He pulled his coat tighter, "Feels like it's getting colder. I think we're going to have to head back soon."

"This has been wonderful," Barbara said. "It's so pretty out here."

"Next year will be even better," Trey promised. "We'll have a fire going in the fireplace in the house!"

"Let's not get ahead of ourselves." Barbara warned. "The future isn't promised."

"It's hopeful," Trey countered. He knelt down to untie her skates. "And I am a very hopeful man." Trey assured.

"You know," Caitlyn said. "You don't have to drive all the way back to my house, Barbara can come with us." She offered.

Trey shook his head, "Nope, this is a *date*, and I intend to get the whole deal." He smiled up at Barbara. "I'm glad you came out today."

"So am I," she answered. "I do love it here."

"In a few months, I'm going to need your help," he said. "The house is going to need a woman's touch, and I want that touch to be yours."

"I have no experience with decorating a house," she warned. "I've lived in convents, remember? You might not like what I come up with."

"I trust you." He insisted. "Besides, you're better with historical stuff than I am. If I want landmark status, we need to use authorized papers and colors. And I think you've a better eye for that than I have."

THE TWO CARS PULLED into the O'Hara drive just as the snow began to fall. Trey and Barbara walked behind the other couple toward the stairs, slowly taking their time. "She still isn't sure of me," Trey said pointed ahead to Caitlyn.

"She's got mother hen syndrome." Barbara said lightly. "It's kind of nice most of the time." After years of convent life where she hadn't had anyone who really cared and looked after her, Barbara enjoyed the feeling of being valued by someone.

"I guess when you've never had it," Trey drew her closer to his side. "I can't imagine the life you've led."

"I wouldn't call it life," Barbara answered, enjoying the closeness he wanted to share with her. IT was unexpected and appreciated. "It's existence only." A sadness swept over her. "I wonder at times like now, this holiday, what my parents were like. What did we do together?"

"We're going to get the answers," Trey promised, "when we do, we'll make sure you never feel alone again."

"I want to feel," she said stopping her steps. "I want to *feel*, happy, sad, good, bad... I want to feel Trey, not just guard myself so I don't get punished."

"Does the Bishop know about that incident?" He asked quietly.

"I'm not sure." She answered. "I've a lot of questions for him as well as others. However, he wasn't in charge when I was turned over to my Grandmother, I don't know what he is aware of. We still haven't heard from my guardian, and I've a feeling that when we do, it won't be good news."

Trey nodded, pursed his lips, and then said, "I think you need a lawyer."

"It has occurred to me," she nodded in agreement.

"Caitlyn's dad is good," he said. "But I doubt he's ever dealt with anything like this."

"I intended to talk to him about this after Christmas," she confessed. "If he thinks he can handle it, I'll ask him to. If not, I'll ask him to recommend someone he trusts."

"Barra," he warned. "This could be expensive, and we have no idea of what funds the guardians have kept for you or from you. If you need money, I'll make you a loan."

She smiled crookedly, "A loan?"

"I'd give you the money outright, but I didn't think you'd take it." He explained logically.

"You read me better than most people do," she admitted. "I wouldn't take money outright; a loan means I can pay you back."

Trey smiled, "You've been on your own a long time," he shrugged. "I wouldn't want to take away your independence. I like the idea of a woman who can hold her own."

"Hey, you two," Jason shouted from the porch. "Quit dawdling! There's a storm coming!"

Barbara extended a hand to Trey, "He's going to have kittens."

"He doesn't trust me," Trey teased. "Because he's a guy!"

"This has been a perfect day," she said as they walked up the walkway. "Thank you so much."

"Just one of many to come, my love." He said, placing an arm about her shoulders. "I want you to live your life, fully."

"Me too," she answered. "Four years ago, when I came here, I had no idea of what my life was going to be. I was so empty."

"One day at a time, Barra." He warned as they stepped up on the porch. "You've got good instincts, trust them."

"I will," she promised as he bent to kiss her.

JASON STOOD AT THE door, watching as Trey pulled out of the drive. "Good thing he doesn't have far to go," he said. "They are calling for the storm to get heavy. I wonder if there's going to be anyone at Church tonight."

"We won't be," his father said from the parlor where he was adding a log to the fire. "I'm not driving in a snowstorm. We don't have anyone singing in the choir tonight, and the fire is keeping this room much too cozy to leave and chance the roads."

Mrs. O'Hara was bringing in a tray of warm cider. "How was the pond?"

"Lovely," Caitlyn said as she took her mug. "Trey served some hot chocolate out at the pond."

"That young man has taken on a lot of responsibility," Mr. O'Hara said. "His father is very proud of him for what he's doing."

"Saving a bit of history?" Barbara suggested.

"That, and his treatment of Mr. Morgan," Mr. O'Hara said. "I know a bit about the bargain they struck, and the price of the orchard; our firm handled the transaction. Everyone here knows the old man would have made more selling it to a land realtor but selling it to keep the orchard intact... Trey has earned a lot of respect for buying the orchard from the community."

"He's got a lot of plans," Barbara said.

"Improvements that won't take away from the charm," Caitlyn nodded. "I wasn't sure how I felt about the old man selling."

"A lot of places are being swallowed up," Jason said. "If dad hadn't bought and leased out the entire farm here, who knows what would sit here?"

"Ticky-tacky houses," Barbara repeated Trey's words.

"Exactly," Jason said making a grand gesture. "Ticky-tacky houses!"

"Trey said he couldn't stand one more ticky-tacky enclave," Caitlyn said. "I agree. There's enough, you need parks and green spaces, and farms and orchards."

"Agriculture isn't hip," Jason said taking a mug of cider, "Most young people are looking for something easy. Hell, half the girls I dated before I went into the service couldn't even cook, Caiti."

"Most of the girls you dated don't even want to go on living in Danbury." Caitlyn counted. "Marsha Drake moved to the city the moment she could."

Barbara listened, feeling this litany had been played out time and again. It felt as if brother and sister agreed but had to come at it from opposite ends. She sipped her mug of cider and observed the family dynamic.

SIGN OF THE RAVEN

Jason took a seat on the sofa, next to his father. "I'm glad you didn't break up the farm."

"There are still farmers in the area," Mr. O'Hara stated, "they would like to keep the family farms going. To do that, they need land to plant."

"Danbury used to have more farms," Jason argued. "Twenty years ago, there was this building explosion. Now there are farms, but not as many, and the shops and mills have been replaced by boutiques."

"Tim's dad hated being part of the construction of the mini malls and boutiques," Caitlyn lamented. "But he's got people to pay, and bills…"

"Progress," Jason lamented.

"I didn't think the area looked that bad," Barbara said. "But I'm still relatively new to the area."

"What you see," Mr. O'Hara said softly, "is a compilation of compromise. When I bought this farm a lot of farms were being swallowed up for subdivisions and tracks of condos and townhouses. Some of us, who grew up here saw what was happening and grew worried. We didn't want our small-town life to be absorbed or destroyed or even engulfed. We wanted our children to experience what we had growing up, to have open spaces and fresh air and places to run and feel free."

"That's why the County Board set up ordinances," Mrs. O'Hara nodded.

"That didn't stop some of the farmers from selling out," Jason grumbled. "I might not be Trey Lochwood's greatest fan, however I'm glad he had the sense to see Morgan's Orchard for the jewel it is."

"So, what is this rivalry you two have going?" Barbara asked.

"Who said we were rivals?" Jason demanded.

"Trey," Barbara answered without a blink.

"Oh." Jason seemed uncomfortable. "How honest of him."

"He said it never extended to girlfriends," Barbara added. "Is that true?"

Jason's face colored. "It's true we never went after the same girl, not at the same time."

"What started it?"

Caitlyn laughed, "A foot-race at the county fair," she snitched. "Trey beat Jason, who was Danbury's fastest runner."

"A foot-race?" Barbara shook her head. "Really?"

Mr. O'Hara nodded, "Three years running, until Trey moved on to the steeple chase." He pointed an accusing finger at his son, "Then this one had to have a horse to compete."

"I nearly won the one year," Jason said defensively.

"Nearly?" His mother turned on him. "You damn near killed that poor horse."

"It got rough," Jason said to Barbara.

"No," His father countered, "*you* got rough, and you were disqualified, and I sold the horse to protect it from your bad sportsmanship!"

Jason looked ashamed, "I was wrong," he admitted. "It wasn't the horses fault I lost; it was mine."

"Poor horse," his mother lamented.

"And because of *him*, none of the rest of us were able to get a horse." Caitlyn accused.

"Horses are a big responsibility," her father stated. "None of you were ready for that."

"I said I was wrong," Jason repeated.

"That doesn't explain why you feel this rivalry." Barbara stated.

"I don't know," Jason admitted. "He gets under my skin."

"This one is used to being the biggest, fastest and best." His mother said pointing. "He won all sorts of trophies at school."

"I'm not like that now," Jason said firmly. "I depend on my brothers in arms. It's teamwork that gets things done."

"Took the US Marines to bang that into his thick skull," his father teased. "And there is still room for improvement."

Barbara looked beyond them to the deepening storm outside, "This place is lovely," she commented quietly. "You've all made it so... homey."

"You should have seen it when we started," Mrs. O'Hara laughed lightly. "It's lovely now, but when we came in, the farmer had started a renovation and quit."

"We all learned drywalling," Jason teased.

"Good thing I'm a good lawyer and make a lot of money," Mr. O'Hara said. "Because this place ate it by the bushels!"

Caitlyn turned the Christmas tree on and turned the lights in the room on low. "Isn't that just beautiful?"

The tree, the room, the storm outside, it was all amazing to Barbara. "This is home," she nodded.

"I'm sorry you don't have memories of your parents," Mrs. O'Hara said for the thousandth time.

"Me too," Barbara nodded. "That's why I'm making the most of these memories." She moved to the large picture window that looked out over the lawn. "This is what I will build on."

CHRISTMAS MORNING, the storm had passed, leaving a blanket of undisturbed snow. The view from Caitlyn's room was one of pastoral splendor. Caitlyn was not as early to rise as Barbara, who was sitting on the window seat enjoying the sunrise on the snow.

"Don't you know how to sleep in?" Caitlyn muttered.

"I don't want to miss a moment of this," Barbara whispered back. Being here was different from being at the convent. Caitlyn's family wasn't overly religious, they didn't fear eternal damnation if they missed a religious holiday. With the storm gone they might make the eleven o'clock service.

Barbara dressed and went down to the kitchen to see if anyone was up yet. She found Mrs. O'Hara sitting in the kitchen with a cup of coffee. "Morning," she said. "Is everything alright? You're up early."

"I'm fine," Mrs. O'Hara assured her. "It's years of getting up at the crack of dawn for the holidays, I can't help myself; I'm up before the old rooster is."

"I understand that," Barbara poured a cup of coffee for herself and joined her friend's mom. "At the convent if I got to sleep until six it was like sleeping in. Most morning the nuns were up by five, and I was expected to join in morning vespers even during holidays."

Mrs. O'Hara frowned, "It's not the picture of what most people think convent life is." Her voice sounded pained. "No child should go through what you did. Spending your entire life cloistered. Just thinking about it, I want to shake your guardian."

"I'm sure there are kids who suffered far more than I did." Barbara said reasonably, "I was safe, and I was educated... not as well as perhaps others, but I made sure I got what I needed in the education department." She looked about the kitchen, "Being here, with you all, is a different kind of education."

"An education? Here?" Mrs. O'Hara giggled. "You must be joking."

"No," Barbara said firmly. "Here, I've learned how a family really functions. I've learned what sharing is, what caring is. I've learned how brothers and sisters behave with each other out of the public eye. I've gained so much insight into what makes a family tick! How husbands and wives get on, how they blend. Here, I've learned what it is I want for myself. That's why I won't make you all targets."

"We love you so," Mrs. O'Hara reached out a hand, "As if you were our own blood."

"Jason says he likes having an orphan in the family." Barbara laughed. "I know he's teasing, but sometimes the way he says things..."

"He's got no tact, that boy," his mother complained. "I raised him better than that." She lamented.

"He's real." Barbara countered. "I like that he treats me like he treats Molly and Caitlyn. Makes me feel like a real part of the family." She sipped her coffee, "Is there anything you need me to do?"

SIGN OF THE RAVEN

"Not just yet," Mrs. O'Hara said. "All the sides were done yesterday, and the bird is in the oven." She pointed to the old stove. "I've got breakfast ready to set up on the sideboard when the rest of the family gets up." She smiled, "We can just sit here and enjoy our coffee."

"I want to thank you," Barbara said softly. "For including me in your family holidays."

"It's been a pleasure to host you," Mrs. O'Hara said. "You've become part of this family."

"I love this house, this family," Barbara confessed.

Mrs. O'Hara watched her, "I wish I could give you the gift of memory," she mused. "So that you could remember your parents and how it was before."

"That's the nicest thing anyone has ever said." Barbara whispered. "It would be lovely."

Mrs. O'Hara nodded, "Have you talked to my husband yet?"

Barbara shook her head, "I thought I'd wait until after today, give the holiday its own time. Then I'll talk to him. I don't want him to feel pressured."

"OH, he won't let you," Mrs. O'Hara assured. "If he feels this is something he cannot do, he'll say so."

"It's asking a great deal," Barbara warned. "I'm not even sure how I'll be able to pay for it."

"There are too many lose ends, and blind allies in your life," Mrs. O'Hara agreed handing her mug to Barbara to refill. "Not knowing anything about your past, or your family finances. Or just what your guardian has been up to…"

"I know," Barbara had her own feelings of distrust about what had been done in her name. "Not knowing where my parents are buried, or if I have family on my father's side… It's enough to test one's metal."

"That your own grandmother didn't take you to the funeral," Mrs. O'Hara complained.

"I have no memory of her, none," Barbara reminded, "it's as if I lived in a bubble."

"Do you remember anything?"

"I don't know," she shook her head, "I don't know what's a dream, or what is real." Barbara had begun to keep a journal; one she'd not even told Mrs. O'Hara about. In it she put down what was fleeting memories. Things she didn't want to lose to time, things that she feared were important facts to follow in her quest to find herself.

"Whatever happens," Barbara said, "I will always hold the memory of this house, and this family. You have saved me."

"Or dragged you into our insanity," teased her friend's mother.

JUST BEFORE DINNER the phone rang, Jason called Barbara to it. "It's that Lochwood boy." He grumbled. "Tell him not to call at dinner time."

Barbara suppressed a giggle, "Hi, Trey," she said. "Merry Christmas."

"Merry Christmas," he retorted in return, "I was wondering if you're free for lunch tomorrow."

"I don't have plans," she said.

"I'd like to bring you with me to visit Mr. Morgan." He told her. "I've a gift for him and I thought you'd like to meet him."

"Lovely," she agreed.

"It's a date," he said before he ended the call.

THE NEXT DAY AT ELEVEN, Trey pulled into the O'Hara drive. He waved at her as he came up to the porch. "How's my girl?" he called out as she came out the door.

"Fine, how are you?"

"Pretty good," he said with a smile. "Did you get a lot of nice things for Christmas?" He teased.

"I did," she teased back, "and you?"

"I got the best," he said coming up the porch in a bound. "I got you." He embraced her and held her close. "Best gift of all."

"Silly man," she hugged him back.

"You're letting cold air in," complained Jason. "Lochwood," he greeted Trey curtly.

"Jason," Trey nodded back, as he stepped inside the house. "I hear Laura Cruikshank is looking for you."

Jason stopped, turned back, and looked at Trey, "Thanks for the warning."

"Don't mention it," Trey said before turning to Barbara, "Make sure you bundle up," he warned. "It's going to get colder."

"I've got a new sweater that Mrs. O'Hara made for me," she nodded and ran off to get her sweater and her coat. When she returned Tim was standing in the door waiting with Trey.

"Barb!" he shouted.

"Tim," she shouted back.

Trey laughed, "Come on, sweetheart, Mr. Morgan is waiting." He held out his hand to her.

Once in the car Barbara asked, "Who is Laura Cruikshank?"

Trey kept his eyes on the road, "Local female barracuda," he answered. "She's had her hooks out for several guys, Jason is at the top of her list."

"Are you one?" she asked.

"Not me, I'm not her type, too unconventional in her words. I had the nerve to disagree with a statement she made. Jason was politer and got himself on her list of candidates for husband material. His folks having money didn't hurt."

"Jason says your folks have money," she argued.

"But I'm not a *nice* boy," he said. "I'm also not the kind who lets a woman ride rough shod over me."

"And Jason is?" her voice squeaked.

"So, Laura thinks; but she'd be wrong."

Barbara stared at him, "Who says you're not a nice boy?"

Trey smiled, "Protective, aren't you? Well, sweetheart, I have a bad reputation, I have no idea how I got it."

"But you've been wonderful to me," she defended.

"I'm in love with you," he reminded her.

"In love?" she repeated. "Trey... you never said..."

"Oh, didn't I? I thought I said something about falling in love and getting married," he teased. "Sweetheart, I haven't seriously looked at or dated anyone since meeting you."

"You said..."

"I said, yes, I dated, but not *seriously*." He acknowledged. His smile widened. "You think I'd give a Thor hammer to just anyone?"

She fingered the pendant, "No."

"I didn't think saying the words out loud at the time was..." he paused looking for the right phrase. "I didn't think it was the right time. I didn't want to scare you off, I wanted you to agree to date me. I figured you'd pick up on the rest in good time; after all, you're a smart girl."

"You love me?"

"That I do," he nodded.

"You don't even know me," she argued.

"I know more about you, than you do," he contended. "Besides, I intend to get to know you very well by the time we get married."

"Married?" she squeaked again.

"Of course, married." He laughed. "We are perfect for one another."

"You're crazy."

"About you." He nodded. "Don't worry, Barra." He said. "I plan on us both being on the same page by then." He sounded pleased with himself.

"Nice of you to let me know," she wasn't cross, mostly she was amused.

"I thought so," he agreed. "Now, let me get you caught up on old man Morgan," he suggested. "His daughter Betty is visiting, and she's decent, it's Mary and young Morgan Jr who cause him problems. He's pretty set in his ways, don't be dismissive of him. He's as observant as a hawk! He most likely will call you girly, it's not insulting, it's just his way."

"Go on," she listened.

"He's nearly eighty-five, but he's as sharp as a tack. He knows all the history of this valley, and of the surrounding counties. His knowledge of orchards and making cider and apple jack is amazing. He is one of the most respected orchardmen in the state! His orchard in its heyday was award winning," Trey said. "The cottage he's living in was his grandmother's house while he was a kid, and his father's gran's before that."

"So, he knows everything, and everyone," Barbara said. "I take it he has his own furnishings from the big house."

"He kept things he liked, gave his kids what they wanted, and redid the cottage with his stuff. I bought the rest with the house. The cottage is all on one level, no stairs up and down." Trey nodded. "I don't have to worry about him taking a fall."

"Sounds good," Barbara said, "And does he know you're not going to charge him rent?"

"OH, hell no!" Trey warned. "If he thought I was giving him charity he'd blow a fuse. I plan on using his so-called rent to make sure the cottage has what he needs, including a visiting nurse."

"Thanks for the heads up, I promise not to blow it." She teased.

"You have more tact than anyone I know," he praised. "He's going to really like you."

"I hope so," she said, and meant it.

A short time later when they drove up to the cottage, Barbara saw it was decorated. "Did he do that?"

"No," Trey sighed, "I did." He shrugged. "I thought the old boy would enjoy them."

"And did he?"

Trey shrugged, "He didn't tear them down."

Barbara laughed.

Trey came around to her side of the car after he parked and opened her door. "Shall we?" he offered her his arm.

"Let's," she nodded taking the arm.

Betty opened the door; Barbara could see she was nearly Caitlyn's mother's age. She was an average height woman, with graying brown hair, and pleasant blue eyes. She smiled at them. "Dad is so excited about this visit," she assured them as she ushered them in. "He's waiting in the parlor."

Trey led Barbara in, "Mr. Morgan, we're here." He said in a clear voice, not too loud, but strong enough to be heard. "I want you to meet Barbara, my girl."

The white-haired gent in the wingback chair looked up, his eyes were the same shade of blue as his daughter's. "Ah, Lochwood," he said reaching out a hand. "Good of you to come and visit," he turned to Barbara, "And who is this pretty young thing?"

"Barbara Gowan," Trey repeated. "My girlfriend."

"Gowan?" Mr. Morgan pushed his glasses up his nose, and looked at her for a long moment, "You don't look like any of the Gowan's I know."

At first, she was stunned to hear that Mr. Morgan knew anyone named Gowan. "I'm not from here," Barbara said, almost apologetically. "I grew up over in Stanhope."

Mr. Morgan studied her face, "Gowan you say?" he shook his head. "You've the look of one of the Ramsey family." He nodded, keeping his eyes on her. "Yes, the shape of that face, the eyes, that nose... You're a Ramsey or my name isn't William Morgan!"

Barbara was fascinated, "Are you sure?" She and Trey exchanged glances, Trey had more than once commented that he didn't think Gowan was her real name.

"The Gowan clan are proud of their pretty faces," Morgan said, scornfully. "They have a habit of marring pretty wives and keeping their bloodline blemish free. All but one, that comes to mind." He motioned for them to be seated. "She was a wild one," he laughed. "Caused her mother more heartache with her running about and keeping company with a man the Gowan's didn't approve of."

"Why?" Barbara asked. "Why didn't they approve of him?"

"He wasn't a conventional lace-curtain Irish Catholic." Mr. Morgan explained. "He was a wild blooded young buck from the Ramsey clan out of Scotland. Not a man arrogant, snobbish, Katherine Gowan wanted her perfect little Mary to be running about with."

Barbara blinked, turned to Trey, "My mother's name was Mary."

"How long ago was this?" Trey asked Mr. Morgan.

"Twenty, maybe twenty-two years ago or so," the old man said. He looked at Barbara, "You don't have the fine build of the Gowan, or the oh so soft features, if you don't mind me observing. You're built a wee bit sturdy, and you're not tall and waiflike."

"No," Barbara acknowledged. "I'm not tall, or a waif."

Mr. Morgan snorted, "I remember when Mary Gowan ran off and married that wild Roan Ramsey. What a stir it caused in at least six counties! Old man Gowan was trying to entice his wild daughter to settle down and marry a proper Irish Catholic boy. He paraded them before her for months, and what a parade it was. She'd have none of it! Along came Roan, with his dark devil eyes, and his dark gypsy good looks and his deep voice... and promises of earthly delights..." He leaned forward, "Stole her away in the dead of night, he did. He married her and there wasn't a thing the old man could do about it. She was of age, and consent, and what a row it caused."

Barbara could feel her cheeks flush, "Did they have children?"

"I recall hearing they had a wee little girl," he tapped his chin with long fingers. "The old man refused to see his daughter or his grandchild and died shortly after the baby was born. His wife raged that it was her daughter's fault the old man died. What a scandal, she blamed the girl when that old man was fond of his liquor and his cigars. His doctor told him to stop, but he was hell bent on doing what he wanted. And they wondered where Mary got her stubborn streak. Katherine shouted for her to get out of the funeral home! Made a scene, in front of God and everybody, including a Bishop that was related to them. There she stood with her two sons, the no-good sons of.... And that poor girl, and her husband and baby being treated as if they had nailed Christ to the cross. I remember it as if it were yesterday." He shook his head at the memory. Barbara could only imagine the scene. "They left the wake and didn't return for the burial."

He looked at Barbara, "Shame of it was, Roan loved Mary with all his heart, even offered to become a catholic. As I heard tell. His father welcomed that girl into their family. Said she was the saving of his son, bought them a fine house in Clarks Town, and gave Roan a job in the family business."

"Family business," Barbara repeated.

"Ramsey Lumber," Morgan nodded. "One of the Ramsey businesses. From what I hear that family branches out as often as they propagate." He chuckled. "Young Roan opened a little side business, hired himself a good cabinet maker. Ramsey fine wood cabinets and tables. And then," he paused, his face went somber. "It all came to a horrible end, on a road not far from here, on a winter's night." He took a deep breath, "But you don't want to hear about that..."

"Yes, I do," Barbara said quietly, "I want to know what happened to them, the family."

Betty stared at her, "You're not from here," she asked.

"No, I grew up in Stanhope." Barbara repeated. She looked back at Mr. Morgan, "I grew up in a convent school, please go on."

Morgan gripped the arms of his chair, "Roan was taking his Mary to an annual ball," he said.

"The Solstice Ball?" Trey asked.

"They called it the Christmas Ball back then," Morgan nodded, "they were coming from their home in Clarks Town. Back then it was the social event of the area, people from six counties came to celebrate." He looked out the window, "There had been an early snow that year, it had snowed on Thanksgiving, and several times after that. That night there was a wet snow falling, and the roads were slick. Even so, there has always been some questions as to what happened."

Barbara leaned forward, "Please, go on."

He stared at her, "I see Roan in your eyes," he said, nodded and continued. "The report that was filed said a truck cut them off, side swiped the car. It rolled down a hill, over and over and over." He closed his eyes, "Poor Mary was like a broken china doll when they found her, she'd been thrown from the car. Her seatbelt failed, looked like it had been torn. Roan wasn't much better, but he was found in the car. Both were dead before they got to them." Mr. Morgan gripped the arms again, "Suddenly there were police everywhere, out of nowhere." He sounded angry. "But no truck, it never stopped."

"What happened to their little girl?"

Morgan frowned, "She vanished that night, much like Mary's body did from the morgue. Her mother claimed her body, and left Roan there to rot. From what I heard; Mary was buried in a private ceremony in the family crept within hours."

"And Roan?" Barbara asked.

"The next day the officials remembered to call his father," Mr. Morgan shook his head, "Several officers lost their positions in a scandal. It wasn't as if the Ramsey's were not known, it was an insult that wasn't to be tolerated. You see, the Irish clans had power here, but so did the Scots, and Ramsey was a powerful man. When the old man went to the house his son lived in the night of the accident, he found only the housekeeper there, weeping and saying she couldn't stop them that the police had come and taken the wee child away. He was smart and called in the State Police, didn't trust the locals not to be bought up by the Gowan's."

Trey reached out his hand, taking Barbara's, "I don't believe in coincidence," he told her.

"Neither do I," she said. "Mr. Morgan, what did Mr. Ramsey do?"

"He hired deceives, offered a ransom, and threatened the Gowan widow." He answered. "Had the house of that old witch watched day and night until she died. I suppose she took the secret of what she did with the child to her grave. I know for a fact, the little girl never surfaced at her Grandmother's house."

"Thank you," Barbara said.

Mr. Morgan studied her face. "I'd keep this to myself for a bit if I were you," the old man warned. "Some of Mary's brothers are still alive last I heard, and were I the child of Mary Gowan, I'd want to stay alive."

She nodded. "Good advice." She leaned forward and kissed his cheek. "Thank you, Mr. Morgan."

TREY LOOKED AT HER once or twice while taking her back to the O'Hara house. "Say something."

"I don't know what to say."

"Why didn't you ask about the branding?" Trey asked. "He might have known about it...."

"If what he says is true," Barbara looked ahead, "my parents were murdered, and... and what he knows could put him in danger. I don't want anyone else to die, Trey."

"What are we going to do?" he asked.

SIGN OF THE RAVEN

"We?"

"We are in this together," he assured her, "I'm not letting you go through this alone!"

"When we get to Caitlyn's, would you come in with me to talk to Mr. O'Hara? I'm not sure I can tell him this without... making it sound like something out of an old movie."

"I'll stay as long as you need me to," he nodded.

Barbara looked at him, "Barbara Ramsey?"

"We don't even know if Barbara is your real name," he reminded her. "Let's take this one step at a time. Mr. O'Hara will know what we should do."

CHAPTER 6.

Mr. O'Hara sat in his study with Trey and Barbara, listening to their tale without interruption. Barbara looked at him, "What should we do?" she asked.

"I remember when that accident happened," he murmured. "I knew of Roan Ramsey, everyone in the county did. I didn't know him personally. However, he was something of a legend back then." He steepled his fingers as he leaned on his desk, "His father turned the county upside down trying to find his baby granddaughter." He looked over at Barbara. "For now, you say nothing to no one, not even Caiti." He warned resolutely. "Not a word."

Barbara nodded, "I won't."

He looked at Trey, who said, "My lips are sealed."

"I'm going to look for information, as to the name of the Ramsey child. And with your permission, I'm going to look into your records, from the convent school." He said. "We'll go from there."

"Be careful," she warned. "If what Mr. Morgan didn't clearly say is true, my parents were likely murdered."

"We'll get to the bottom of this," Mr. O'Hara promised. "Until we do, not a word."

Trey and Barbara walked out of the study and headed to the door. "I'm sorry this is so muddled," he said as she saw him out. "Who knew this day was going to be turned upside down?"

"Ever since solstice," Barbara confided, "I've had an uneasy feeling that something was about to happen. This isn't what I expected, but something tells me it's the tip of the iceberg."

Trey touched her face, tipping her chin upward, "We're in this together. No more facing things alone," he assured her.

"Trey," she moaned, "I've got such a bad feeling about this."

"I know," he said. "But you're not in this alone."

"I don't want anyone else to be hurt," she said. "If what Mr. Morgan said is half true..." she shook her head. "This is all so horrid, what kind of people are my family?"

"All the more reason I don't want you in this alone!" He said. "Any word from your guardian?"

"Not a peep," Barbara whispered, "that's not unusual. None of them ever acknowledged my birthday, or the holidays."

"I would think you'd be hearing from their lawyer," Trey warned. "Relinquishing your care is going to be problematic as you didn't take the veil as they intended."

"Who does that?" she complained. "Plan out someone else's existence?"

"Someone who thinks they have you under their thumb," Trey leaned on the door. "Barra, I think we might have to have a talk to that Bishop, the one that forced your guardian's hand."

"I was planning on contacting him," she nodded. "I thought I could wait until spring when my degree is finished."

"I think we should sit down, and write up a list of who, what, when and where!" Trey shook his head. "I'll pick you up for dinner Saturday," he promised. "I'll be here at six."

"I'll be ready," she promised back. She kissed him and sent him on his way. When she turned around Caitlyn and Tim were standing behind her. "Hi, guys." She said.

"What's going on?" Caitlyn demanded. "Why were you and Trey huddled with daddy?"

"I can't tell you all the details," Barbara said. "I'll tell you this, things from my past are about to hit the fan."

Tim whistled, "Anything we can do to help?"

"I don't know," Barbara shook her head, "Everything is so far from what I had thought or planned."

Caitlyn came forward, wrapping her arms about her, "We're here for you," she said in Barbara's ear.

"I know that you are." Barbara answered, putting her arms in turn about her friend. "Knowing that is what makes this easier to live through." She looked over at Tim, "You two were my first friends, ever."

"We'll be with you for life," Tim promised. "No matter what."

THE DAY BEFORE CLASSES resumed was chaos on campus. Barbara hauled the bag on her shoulder up the stairs to the floor where her dorm room was. She placed the key in the door, and it wouldn't turn. She checked, it was the right key, and she tried again. Still it wouldn't turn. A moment later the door opened, and her roommate stared at her.

"What are you doing here?" She asked.

"I live here," Barbara reminded her with a wistful smile.

"Not anymore," the other girl said, and pointed to the wide open and empty closet, "You moved out."

"When?" Barbara stepped in, looking at the empty space where her few belongings had hung.

"I got back yesterday, there was a letter of eviction on your desk," the girl pointed to the desk that Barbara used. "I went out for dinner and when I got back the letter and your things were gone. They changed the lock and gave me a new key." She showed her the key.

"This is damned strange," Barbara said. "My tuition covers everything until spring." She looked in the desk, everything was gone. "You say there was a letter of eviction?"

"Yeah," the other nodded. "You mean you didn't take your things? Someone just can come in and pack you up?"

"Not according to the rules," Barbara pulled her cellphone out of her pocket and hit speed dial. "Mr. O'Hara, I think I need a lawyer and the police. I've been evicted, and my belongings have vanished." She quickly explained what had happened.

"Go to the bursar's office," he instructed. "I'll meet you there in half an hour with the police."

Barbara turned to her once roomie, "I'm sorry we never got to know one another," she held out her hand. "I have my doubts that I'll be coming back."

The other girl took her hand, "I thought you were a fantastic roomie," she said in return. "You never took things, you were polite and quiet, and you kept your side neat as a pin." She shook the hand firmly. "I'm going to miss you." She shrugged, "But it's kind of hard to get to know people when you're on the move. My courses require me to go into the field at the drop of a hat." She smiled, "I wish you well."

"You too," Barbara shouldered her overnight duffle back and headed back down to the campus quad. She moved quietly toward the offices where other students were getting new rooms assigned and rescheduling classes. She waited outside the Bursar's office, and a few minutes later Mr. O'Hara showed up with the county sheriff who had an odd amused expression on his face.

"I have warrants sworn out," Mr. O'Hara said. "Just in case."

"I can't imagine what's going on," Barbara complained.

"Can't you?" Mr. O'Hara didn't seem as surprised as she was. "I've a feeling your guardian is behind this."

"But why?" she heard her voice go up an octave.

The sheriff opened the door, "Let's go find out why," he suggested, with an amused grin. Barbara found that a bit odd, as if a private in joke was being played, and she'd been left out in the dark.

They marched into the Bursar's outer lobby and requested to see the Bursar. The woman behind the counter looked at Barbara's student ID, pushed a few keys on the computer and announced, "You're no longer a student here, I'll take that ID." She reached for it.

"No, you will not," Barbara said firmly. "Since when am I no longer a student?"

"You were *expelled* during the winter break," the woman said in a testy tone.

"For what reason?" Barbara inquired. "My scholarship was confirmed and has paid all my tuition and fees until spring when I was to graduate."

The woman behind the desk looked at her, and then at the men standing with her. "I am not at liberty to give the reasons." She turned off the computer screen, "You'd have to take that up with the Bursar, and he's busy. You'll have to make an appointment."

"Is he free to be arrested?" the Sheriff inquired with humor.

"I don't find that funny," the woman snapped.

"I doubt he will either, but you better get him out here now or I'll go in there after him." He warned.

Barbara thought the woman was going to object, but she picked up the phone and when someone answered she said. "There's a police-officer here to see you, sir."

The door of the inner office flew open, "What is the meaning of this?" The Bursar demanded.

"Why was I expelled, and where are my belongings?" Barbara demanded over his fuss.

"The reason for your expulsion was listed in the eviction letter we sent you." The Bursar said hotly. "I suggest you read it."

"I never received it," she crossed her arms. "I've been off campus for the holiday. I've only just returned to find my belongings removed and my key not working."

The Bursar looked at the men standing behind her, "What reason did you have to involve the police."

"The sheriff is here to protect my rights, just as my lawyer is," Barbara answered. "Where are my belongings?"

"I have no idea," he fidgeted. "And I don't care, you are no longer one of our students."

"Who did you allow in my room?" She demanded.

He glared at her, "You are no longer a student, I don't answer to you."

"The judge might see that differently," warned Mr. O'Hara. "So, why don't we just find out. Officer, arrest the Bursar."

"I will not be harassed," the Bursar complained.

"But you don't mind harassing a student," Mr. O'Hara said.

"She," the Bursar pointed at Barbara with venom in his eyes, "is not a student here. She never should have been, she perpetrated a fraud!"

"What fraud would that be?" Barbara asked in surprise.

"You are not who you said you are," He spat at her.

"Who am I?" Barbara raised a brow.

Mr. O'Hara nodded at the Sheriff, "I've had enough, arrest this man, and then go and arrest Miss Gowan's guardian. I believe you know where to find her."

Barbara looked at her friend's father, "You know who my guardian is?" When he nodded, she blinked.

"It will be my pleasure," the Sheriff said with a smile, "Lawson, you're under arrest."

"On what charges?" he shouted.

"Allowing a person without authority into my room, for one." Barbara said with a smile. "You see, as of Solstice, my guardian had no authority over me any longer. I am of legal age."

SIGN OF THE RAVEN

The man with the cuffs on his wrists sputtered. "That cannot be!"

"Even with authority, my guardian had no rights in my room, as it was paid for by my scholarship, which had nothing to do with my guardian. The only person who has the right to cancel my scholarship is the Bishop, and I don't think this is his doing. As for fraud, the only persons who pulled a fraud were the system of guardians set up when I was five." Barbara announced.

"You'd make a very good lawyer, ever consider changing your major?" Mr. O'Hara asked with a smile.

"I'd rather teach history." Barbara said. "However, now that is in jeopardy." She looked at Mr. O'Hara. "What could they have done with my belongings?"

"We'll find them," he assured her. "By the time we get to the court to set up a suit, your guardian should be on her way to the courthouse."

"This isn't the way I wanted this to go." Barbara complained.

"It is, what it is," Mr. O'Hara shrugged. "Shall we?" he offered her his arm.

An hour later, sitting in the county courthouse, Mr. O'Hara had a cryptic smile on his face. "You look like you're enjoying this." Barbara whispered.

"I've been working on this since you told me about your meeting with Mr. Morgan." He confessed. "Had the suit already to go, I was certain we were going to need it. I hadn't thought it would go this quickly." He mused. "I had thought they would let you get settled into class before pulling the rug out from under you."

"It's only been a little over a week," she replied. "How could you have gotten that much done?"

"I took Trey up on his suggestion that I look at what he had uncovered. From there, I followed the bread crumb trail." He looked about the courtroom, "This should prove interesting."

Mr. Lawson sat at the table across from them, no longer cuffed, and with a lawyer who didn't look happy at all. He kept whispering in a furious manner. They kept up this whisper banter until the bailiff announced the Judge's entry.

Judge MacAfee strutted in, took his seat, and slammed the gavel down. "What is this?" he put his glasses on and read, as he did, two officers escorted an angry woman who was shouting at them to take the cuffs off her this instant. The Judge looked over his rims, seeing her didn't please him. He placed the complaint down, "Mrs. Byrne, I should have known this had something to do with you."

"Your honor, I have no idea why I've been dragged here," the woman complained.

"Don't you?" he didn't sound convinced. "Don't play coy with me Marilla, it doesn't work on me. Or have you forgotten?"

Barbara turned with a jolt to Mr. O'Hara, the judge and her guardian knew each other. Mr. O'Hara didn't seem disturbed by this at all. He was grinning and enjoying the confrontation. She shook her head and turned her attention back to the judge.

He seemed to be getting ready to speak when the doors of the courtroom bust open and the College's president stormed into the room. "What is the meaning of arresting my Bursar and dragging him into court."

"Good morning, Harold," Mr. O'Hara stood, and said pleasantly. "How are you?"

President Morris turned to Mr. O'Hara and frowned, "You had better have a good explanation for this, O'Hara!"

"It's a dozy," O'Hara promised. "But I don't think you're going to like it, Harold."

Morris turned to the Bursar with suspicion, "What have you done?" he accused.

Lawson had the good sense not to speak.

Barbara looked at the judge, trying to get a read on him. He was an older man, older than Mr. O'Hara, and older than the woman who had been brought in. He was nearly bald, thin, and had a scholarly face. His most prominent feature was his nose, it was long and pointed.

He brought the gavel down and it sounded like thunder. "Order!" he shouted. He put the gavel down, and leaned back in his chair, observing everyone in the room. "Well, ladies and gents, let's see if we can make some sense of this complaint." He looked at Mr. O'Hara, "O'Hara," he greeted him, "you look pleased."

"I love the law," O'Hara said happily. "Always a pleasure to see it in action."

The Judge nodded, not nearly as amused, but not angry. He then turned and looked at the officials from the College, "Gentlemen," he motioned them to stand. "We are going to start with you." He looked at the woman, "Take a seat, Marilla, and wait your turn."

She glared, but quietly took a seat.

"Your honor," the lawyer for Lawson spoke, "this complaint is unfounded and..."

"Be still, I'm not talking to you," the Judge warned. He picked up the complaint, "It says here that you violated the rights of a student, that's a serious charge, Lawson."

"I did no such thing!" He objected. "I was within my rights to terminate her! She is a fraud!"

Harold Morris, the president of the school stared, opened mouthed. Barbara had a feeling this was the first he'd heard of this.

The Judge raised a brow, "Says here you evicted her without notice, and allowed unknown persons to remove her belongings. Is this true?" Lawson and his lawyer were speaking furiously again, the Judge watched and waited. When no answer came, he said, "It's a simple question, Lawson. Did you allow unknown persons to remove her belongings?"

"She was evicted from the dorm," Lawson nodded.

"By unknown persons?" the Judge pressed.

"I cannot answer that," Lawson said.

"Cannot or will not?" the Judge asked.

Barbara looked over at the Bursar, in the four years she'd been attending the College she's only seen the man twice. Even then she hadn't talked to him. He looked unhappy at being asked such direct questions.

Lawson turned to his lawyer, who held up his hands, "Both," Lawson said at last.

The Judge shook his head, made a note on the complaint, and looked at the president of the college, "President Morris," he greeted him cordially. "Were you aware of the actions of your Bursar?"

"Not until this morning," Harold Morris said. "At the moment I don't have a comment, as I have not looked into the matter as *yet*." He then looked from the Bursar over to Marilla Byrne. Who in turn refused to acknowledge him.

"I see," the Judge made another note. He waved Morris to be seated. "And Marilla," he said, his voice turned saccharine. "We come to you. The complaint has you as compliant to the actions of the College." She stood up but said nothing. The Judge waved her to be seated again. He made more notes and turned to Barbara. "You are the complainant?"

"It appears that I am," she stood up.

"I see you have representation," he pointed to O'Hara.

"It seemed reasonable and sound," Barbara nodded.

The Judge hid what appeared to be a grin behind a hand, "Young lady, I'd like to hear from you." He motioned her to come forward. "Bailiff," he directed, "swear her in."

"I object!" Marilla shouted. "You can't believe a word out her lying mouth!"

"Sit down, Marilla!" the Judge ordered. "You'll have your turn to speak."

Barbara paused on her way up to the witness stand. She looked at the woman, she'd never seen her before. It was upsetting, knowing this was her guardian, and she was calling her a liar. She looked at the Judge, he motioned her to come forward. Since Mr. O'Hara hadn't tried to halt her, or the Judge's questioning, she moved forward and into the stand.

"Raise your right hand," the Bailiff directed. He gave her the oath, and she answered.

"I do," she said.

"State your name."

Barbara looked at the judge, "Since I was five, I've been told that my name is Barbara Gowan, and that is the name I have gone by." She said. "However, recently I suspect that's not the case."

The Judge held up a hand to quell the commotion that her words created. "Why do you have such suspicions?"

Barbara looked at Lawson, "Because he said so."

Lawson scrunched down, as if he wished to hide.

The Judge nodded, "And you are the ward of Marilla Byrne?"

"No," Barbara answered, "I turned twenty-one on Solstice, and that ended my being anyone's ward. Mrs. Byrne there may have been my most recent guardian, but I couldn't say as I never met her before today." It was Marilla's turn to look embarrassed.

"How long have you been a ward?" the Judge asked, taking notes.

"Since I turned five, your honor. My first guardian was my Grandmother, Mrs. Gowan." There was a rush of murmuring in the courtroom.

"And how was your relationship with her?" the Judge inquired.

"There wasn't any," Barbara answered. "I never met the lady."

The Judge put down his pen, "I beg your pardon?"

"The night my parents died, I was removed from my home, by force..." Barbara related. "I was taken to the convent School of St. Mary in Stanhope and turned over to the care of Mother Angelica, where I stayed until I was sent to Our Lady of Perpetual Hope in Cortland." She looked over at Mrs. Byrne. "I never met my grandmother or Mrs. Byrne or any of the others who acted as my guardians."

"Surely you met them when you came home for holidays and vacation," the Judge interrupted.

"No, sir," Barbara said, "I stayed at the convent schools year-round."

"But when your parents were buried, surely you met them then." He said.

Barbara looked at him and cocked her head. "I wasn't allowed to attend their burial. I have no idea where my parents are buried. The one time I asked a question about my parents, a Nun hit me so hard, I awoke in the infirmary. I didn't ask again."

Again, a commotion interrupted as three sisters in the habits of the order of the Sisters of Good Hope entered along with the local Bishop who had intervened for Barbara. It was the Bishop who spoke, "I am sorry to interrupt, your honor, we were regrettably late getting started."

Barbara recognized two of the sisters, Mother Mary Clare from Cortland, and Mother Angelica from Stanhope. Barbara's hand went to the arm of the chair she was seated in. She had hoped to never see either woman again.

"Your Eminence," the Judge acknowledged him. "Miss Gowan, here, has just told me that she was a permanent ward of the convents, is that true?"

"I imagine it seemed so to the child," the Bishop said. "She was given over to the Sisters of Good Hope, before I became Bishop. It seems her guardian, her grandmother, wanted nothing to do with her." He shook his head, "When her grandmother, Mrs. Katherine Gowan passed, she was passed on to another guardian, and finally to Mrs. Byrne." He explained.

The Judge made more notes, "Miss Gowan," he said.

"Stop calling her that," Marilla shouted. "She has no right to the name, or to any other name that is decent!" She stood up, "She's nothing but the devil's spawn. A nameless bastard."

"For shame, Mrs. Byrne," the Bishop admonished. "You know that's not true."

"Her mother was never married in the eyes of God!" Marilla accused. "Therefore, that child is a nameless bastard." She repeated the accusation.

"Her parents' marriage was legal and accepted by the state," the Bishop argued.

"Not by the church or her family!" Marilla retorted. "That man stole our Mary, defiled her, and made a mockery of marriage." She glared at Barbara, "Even with years in the convent, this creature cannot be saved. She has no right to that name, or it's benefits, she is nameless."

Barbara looked at her, not feeling hate, not feeling love, not feeling anything. "You're the one who claimed I defrauded the scholarship and the college." It was a calm statement, so coldly delivered, that the woman drew back. Barbara shook her head in disbelieve. "You and the other guardians forced me all my life to use that name, and then you try to take it from me, just when I'm about to graduate? All because I wouldn't take the veil?"

The Bishop glared at Marilla, "I warned you," he said with animosity, "The taking of holy vows is a personal choice. You cannot make it for her. You don't have the right!"

"She shouldn't even exist!" Marilla shouted back at the cleric. "She's an abomination in the eyes of God."

"What is it that I did to you?" Barbara asked.

"You exist." Marilla screamed.

The Judge had been listening to the exchange, he tapped the gavel and the room when as still as the grave. He looked at Barbara, "What kind of life did you have at the convent school?"

Both Mother's Superior looked down.

Barbara looked at the Judge, "One of loneliness," she whispered. "I had no friends, at first I was too young, then the other girls found me too strange, and some of the sisters felt that I didn't belong in the society of young ladies from good families." She looked at the two nuns, she didn't hate them, but there was no love lost there either. "I was given an education, not nearly as complete as the other girls, perhaps the bare minimum. I was never taught the social graces; I think it upset them that I excelled at my studies."

"Go on," the Judge said.

"During the times of Holiday or vacation, I could help in the convent kitchen. I was expected to pray with the sisters, and to observe the great silence. I spent a great deal of time in the library, but when it came to use a computer, I was only allowed to use it for class work. I never had friends or went on outings. I wasn't allowed to go to the Cotillion, my guardian refused to pay for the traditional coming out gown. And because of that, I was also not allowed to graduate with my class." She looked over at the Bishop, "If it were not for his Eminence, I wouldn't have been allowed to accept the scholarship I'd won."

"You had no friends?" The Judge put his pen down.

"Not until I arrived here in Danbury," Barbara answered. "Even then it was hard at first. Because of how I had been cloistered, I was socially awkward." She took a breath, "I didn't know how to dress like the other young people. My guardian refused to pay for a proper wardrobe, the nuns scrambled to find me garments... they pulled things from the poor box, and..." she paused and remembered Caitlyn's words. "What I did have when I arrived here, made me resemble someone in the Goth movement." Barbara sighed, "It's a wonder anyone wanted to befriend me at all."

"Is this true?" the Judge looked at the two sisters sitting in the same row of people as Marilla who was glaring at the judge.

Mother Mary Clare stood up, her arms in the sleeves of her habit, "Yes, your honor. Mrs. Byrne refused our request for funds for the Cotillion gown, and every other effort we made to bring them together." She looked over at Barbara with pity. "She refused to allow us to educate the girl in the simplest of social graces, and demanded we treat her as a postulant." She spoke next to Barbara, "We did our best by you, my child."

The Judge turned to Mother Angelica, "What she said about being struck, and awakening in the infirmary..."

Mother Angelica stood and nodded, "Sister Mary Joseph, whom we later learned was related to the late Mrs. Gowan, was removed from our location after the incident."

"Was a report made?"

Mother Angelica hung her head, "No, we didn't report it, not even to the Bishop. Sister Mary Joseph told us if we did, the funds we'd been given would be taken back and the convent and school would fail."

"My predecessor wouldn't have done a thing if they had reported the incident," Bishop Myer said with disdain, "He too was part of this plot against this child." He shook his head in disgust. "I've only recently learned about most of it," he pointed at Marilia, "when Mrs. Byrne requested the excommunication of this child."

"You did what?" Barbara asked, standing up. Remembering herself, she turned to the Judge, "I'm sorry for my outburst, your Honor."

"Don't be," the Judge said. "I'm finding this entire case outrageous; I don't know how you've managed to turn out this well." He shook his head, "If I wasn't hearing this, firsthand, I'd say it was an outlandish tale." He studied her face. "You did make friends?"

"A few," she answered, "Caitlyn O'Hara, and her boyfriend Tim Boyle were the first, and the longest lasting of the friends I've made here. Through Caitlyn, I became acquainted with her family, and they have included me in most of their holiday celebrations. It was with them I spent this last winter break."

"And when break was over?"

"I arrived at my dorm room to find that my key no longer worked." Barbara explained, "My roommate opened the door and was surprised to find me there, she explained that I have been evicted. She allowed me into the room, and all of my belongings had been removed."

"What did you do next?"

"Before I exited the room, I called Caitlyn's father, Mr. O'Hara who is a lawyer and he suggested that I meet him and the Sheriff at the Bursar's office. When the Bursar refused to answer my questions, Mr. O'Hara had him arrested."

President Morris turned to the Bursar.

"Did you receive a letter of eviction?" the Judge inquired.

"No, sir." Barbara answered. "My roommate said one had been delivered. But when she left the room to go to dinner, it was on my desk. When she returned, the letter and my belongings were gone." She looked over at Mr. Lawson. "When I asked the Bursar, what were the reasons for my being evicted and my scholarship overturned, he told me I had defrauded the college." She looked at the Judge, "From the time I was five, I had been under the impression that my name was Gowan. It was the only name ever used. I grew up using this name, it's on my school records, and on my scholarship. If a fraud has been perpetrated, it has been on me first. I was in good faith, using the only name I knew." She shook her head, "No one had my permission to enter my dorm room. No one had my permission to remove my belongings. Mr. Lawson refused to tell me who took my things, and where."

The Judge looked at Marilla Byrne, "Did you order the removal of this young lady's belongings?"

"She owns nothing," Marilla argued. "Everything in that room was part of the agreement of wardship. Therefore, it was mine to do with as I chose."

"I'm afraid you're wrong," Barbara said. "The rags the nuns sent me to Danbury with are long gone, and I bought the clothes, and the laptop. All the items in the room were mine, not yours. And your wardship of me ended on Solstice."

"You should have taken the veil," Marilla spat. "No one in their right minds would want a devil's spawn like you in their life." She smiled an evil smile, "And when I'm done with you, you'll have no name, no degree, and nothing to stand on."

SIGN OF THE RAVEN

The Judge's gavel silenced Marilla with a shocked look, he leaned forward, "Mrs. Byrne, I want to see the original document of guardianship."

"I refuse," she said. "I don't have to show you a bloody thing!"

"I can put you in jail, Marilla. Just think how the ladies in the Country Club will love that for gossip." He warned.

"That's blackmail, you bastard," she retorted.

"Effect isn't it?" the Judge responded.

Chapter 7.

Marilla and the Judge were at a standoff, and Barbara felt like she was in a nightmare. Mrs. Byrne glared at the Judge, "There's nothing on paper," she said through gritted teeth.

The Bishop's gasp was auditable, as was the gasp from the two Nuns sitting beside him.

Barbara looked at the doors of the courtroom, Trey was entering with a man who looked angry and unmoving. She looked at Mr. O'Hara, who stood and motioned them to join him at the table he sat behind. She didn't know the man, who was older, and graying; however, there was something about him that was familiar. She wondered what O'Hara was up to. Trey handed some legal looking documents to Caitlyn's father.

"Let me get this straight," the Judge leaned back in his seat, gavel in his hand, twirling. "This child was removed from her home, without legal documentation giving you or her grandmother the right to guardianship?"

"Stop acting like a Jackass," Marilla accused. "You know I tried to get documentation."

"I know I refused to be a party to defrauding the legal system," the Judge responded. "Marilla, Marilla, I warned you ten years ago that ever you were up to was going to come back to bite you in the ass."

Barbara frowned. "Ten years ago? My grandmother died ten years so the sisters told me. Mother Angelica made me pray for her

no doubt," the Judge nodded. "You have no idea of what has n, do you?"

o idea of who you are," he mused.

said softly, "Outside of what I've been told over and

that woman," he pointed across the courtroom.

"No, sir, I've never seen her before today." She looked at the sisters with the Bishop. "I know his Eminence, he fought for me to be able to use my scholarship, I know Mother Angelica and Mother Mary Clare, they more or less raised me." She looked back at Mrs. Byrne, "I don't know this woman. You say she's my last guardian and I believe you, but I don't know her. Just as I didn't know my grandmother."

"Marilla, you're an evil wicked woman," the Judge accused, "and your sister, the late Mrs. Gowan was worse."

"Don't speak evil of the dead," Marilla warned. "She did what she had to do, to save her daughter's soul."

Barbara looked at the woman speaking, "Did that include killing my parents?"

The Judge turned and asked, "What did you say?"

"There's been speculation that the accident that took my parent's life, wasn't an accident at all." Barbara whispered. "I know that my parents are dead, even if I wasn't allowed to be at their burial. I know that my mother's name was given to the nuns as Mary Gowan." The man seated by Mr. O'Hara looked up sharply. "I overheard two of the sisters discussing me and they spoke my mother's name."

She took a deep breath, "I know that none of my mother's people wanted me, and that I have no idea of whom my father's people are or what their name is." She looked at the Judge, "But recently, someone said..." she took a deep breath, "I resemble a Ramsey."

"Don't speak that devil name," Marilla shrilly shouted. "You've no right to speak that name or any other."

The gavel fell from the Judge's hand, and he stared. "Ramsey?"

"Yes, sir." She whispered.

The man seated between Trey and Mr. O'Hara stood up, "Can it be?" he asked. "After all these years?"

Marilla ignored him and shouted, "You've no name, you're a bastard child, and you deserve nothing but scorn! We put you in the convent school to curb your evil ways. You will take the veil, or I'll see you dead!"

"Don't make threats in my courtroom," the Judge admonished. "You have no authority here!"

"And you'll have none when I'm done with you," Marilla threatened him. "I warned you ten years ago that my family has power!"

"Had," the Judge said. "When Old man Gowan died, and then his God forsaken wife... his own sons couldn't curry favor with the legal system anymore. Whatever power you think you have, doesn't exist." He looked at Barbara with a much gentler gaze, "You've no reason to fear her, and her empty threats."

"I don't think her threats are empty." Barbara warned, "I think Mrs. Gowan, my grandmother, had my parents killed."

"Your honor," Mr. O'Hara spoke up, in his hand were legal documents, "I have here two records for your inspection, both are birth certificates. One is the very one that his Eminence supplied from the church's records. How this child was registered with the sisters at St. Mary's school."

"Traitor!" Marilla shouted at the Cleric, she moved toward him, but with her hands still cuffed she could not do him damage. "I will never forgive you this!"

"I answer to God," he reminded Marilla, "not to the Gowan family or their relations."

Mr. O'Hara moved forward and handed the papers to the Judge, who said. "Do you have more?"

"A baptismal record that was never recorded in the church records," O'Hara nodded, handing the document up.

"We have reason to believe the birth record and this were forged with full knowledge of my predecessor." The Bishop admitted.

"That's a serious accusation," warned the Judge, he looked at the Bishop, "you agree with Mr. O'Hara?"

SIGN OF THE RAVEN

The Bishop nodded, "When he came to me with the story two weeks ago, I wanted to tell him there was no way it could be true. However, my personal history with the Gowan and Byrne family told me not to rush to judgement. I studied the records personally and gave those to Mr. O'Hara." He glared at Mrs. Byrne, "The Church isn't in the habit of making personal vendettas against innocent children. That she has been raised as a Catholic, without benefit of baptism into our community is a sin against *her*, not by her."

"She's no innocent, she's as dark in the soul as her father." Marilla spat. "Devil's Spawn!"

The Judge looked at Barbara, "Do you have personal identification?"

"I have a social security card," she answered, "and I have a voter registration card, and my student ID." She removed all of them from her wallet and placed them on the Judge's bench.

"A driver's license?" the Judge asked.

"I never was allowed to take the classes, I was told my guardian didn't feel it was something I needed," she answered. "When I arrived here at Danbury, I used the bus system, until my friends drove me where I needed to go."

"You didn't apply for a license here?" the Judge looked at her, perplexed.

"I was afraid to rock the boat," Barbara confessed. "I knew something was wrong, that something about my legal status wasn't right. I had planned on looking into the matter once I was fully emancipated. However, when I arrived here, I was only seventeen, I hadn't yet reached eighteen. I would have needed permission from my guardian to take the driving course, and the funds to pay for it. Something I knew I'd never receive." She didn't need to look; she knew that Mrs. Byrne was seething. "I decided when I arrived here in Danbury, that I would maintain as low a profile as possible. No license, no trouble, no making waves."

"You're an unusual young woman," the Judge remarked.

"I'm on oddity," Barbara agreed. "Recently information has begun to surface, and I was going to pursue it, but only after I had graduated. Forcing me out of my dorm, removing me from my scholarship classes, and making it impossible for me to get information on my belongs... has forced my hand." She looked at Mrs. Byrne. "I want to know who I am, and why they felt they had a right to treat me as if I didn't exist." She didn't flinch when the old woman glared at her, "I want to know where my parents are buried, so I can visit and pay them the homage due them."

"And what makes you believe you're a Ramsey?" Mr. O'Hara said, loud enough for his voice to carry across the entire room, filling it.

Barbara unbuttoned the cuff of her left arm, and rolled up her sleeve, "I'm branded, the Raven." Her arm bore the brand, and a henna wash over the outline filling in the void. "It is a sign used by the Ramsey family."

"Barra," the man seated beside Trey, rose up and said. "Is it you?"

"Mark of the devil!" Mrs. Byrne declared. "Who gave you permission to disfigure yourself?"

"It's a henna wash, Mrs. Byrne, not an ink." Barbara said. "I looked up the technique in a history book. IT's not a devil worship mark, it's an old Celtic mark, to prevent the English from selling off Scottish children." She turned to the Judge, "I love history, don't you?"

"Sir," the Judge addressed the man who was still standing, "Would you come forward, and inspect this mark?"

"With pleasure," he said.

Barbara watched him, he was not a light man, nor was he slight. He was taller than Mrs. Byrne and had a kind but troubled face. He had seen suffering, she thought, and he moved with purpose. His hair was gray, his eyes were dark brown, he offered her a placid smile. "I won't hurt you, child," he promised as his hand reached for her arm. "May I?"

Barbara looked over at Trey, who nodded. "I know," she said. "Go ahead, look."

His touch was gentle, almost clinical, "Do you know the meaning of this mark?"

"It declares me The Raven," she said. "From what I understand it is a mixture of Celtic and Norse runes." She nodded.

He looked into her eyes, "Do you know how it is done?"

She studied him, was he testing her? "I've been told it's done with hot pins; they are in a form and are pressed into the skin, carefully so not to do damage. Then a dye made from specific herbs and plants is introduced. It's not an ink, it's a dye or a stain," she repeated. "But mine was unfinished, I was a baby when this was made, and the follow ups were not done."

The old man smiled, "The follow ups?"

"Each year a new layer of the dye is added, until the entire outline is filled in," Barbara answered.

"The mark of the devil," Mrs. Byrne repeated.

"No," Barbara answered, "it was done by high ranking Celts, in Ireland and Scotland and Wales. It was done by members who had Viking blood, a means of keeping the lines honored. It was a way to prevent the English from breeding us out of existence." She looked at the man inspecting her arm, "The Celts would brand their children, and marry them off in secret to other Celts who were of blended Viking decent."

"Aye, that they would," he answered. "Why did you paint this with Henna?"

"To fill in the area that should have been dyed over the years," she answered. "Henna isn't long lasting, it wears off. I wanted to see what it would have looked like if it had been finished."

"Do you recognize the brand?" the Judge asked.

"Aye, it's my mark," the old man said. "Mary's child carried this mark, put there by my own hand when she was but a year old."

"No," Marilla screamed. "He lies!"

"Mary was my daughter in law," the man said, facing Marilla Byrne. "Roan loved her with all his heart, and she gentled his wild ways. I loved her as if she were my own daughter, and I was honored to have her as family."

"I was told it was unusual for a girl child to bear this mark," Barbara said. "That it is usually given to the first born son."

"It is," the old man agreed. "Mary was fragile, more than anyone knew. When she gave birth to her baby girl, she was told she would never be able to carry another child to term. When the baby reached her first birthday, she asked me to declare her the heir, and the Raven following Roan." He looked at the Judge, "This is Mary and Roan's child. The same child that vanished on that night when their car was run off the road." He nodded, "I am sure of it." He looked back at Barbara, "Your name is Barra Marie Ramsey."

"She's a bastard," Marilla insisted. "The church never sanctioned that marriage! She has no name!"

"Your parents were married by a justice of the peace," the old man said. "And later in a religious ceremony, not Roman, but religious. You are not nameless, nor a bastard, no matter what that foolish old woman says."

"Barra?" she looked over at Trey, "really?"

"I am your grandfather, I am Dane Ramsey, father of Roan." Mr. Ramsey said. "I have turned every stone looking for you, where did they hide you?"

"Where no one would look," Barbara looked over at Marilla, "Katherine Gowan put me in St. Mary of the Dragon with the Sisters of No Hope," she quipped. "Under the name Barbara, Barbara Mary Gowan."

"St. Mary of the Dragon," her grandfather snorted, "Aye, if you don't sound like your father."

"Between Stanhope and Cortland, they kept me hidden," she accused. "So close, and yet so far." She reached across the witness stand to take his hands, "Just knowing I was looked for, makes me feel less alone." She could have wept for joy, "I don't understand how this happened."

"The housekeep tried to stop them," her grandfather said, looking over at the judge before looking back at her. "She said they broke down the door, pulled a gun on her and forced her to watch as you were dragged out of your wee bed."

"I remember a cold hand shanking me," she said. "Everything before that is a flicker." She looked at him, "They didn't even let me keep a picture of my parents. They wanted me to forget my life, my parents, my home."

"Katherine was an evil, spiteful woman." Ramsey nodded. "She left my son to rot in a morgue, while she confiscated the body of her daughter and had it buried in secret. She tried to have the house ransacked, but as soon as you were taken, the housekeeper called me, and I called the law, not the local law, but the state officers. They didn't dare do what they intended." He looked over at the judge, "It took me twenty-four hours to locate my son's remains."

"Why?" Barbara asked. "Why did she hate me so much? She was my grandmother."

"Because you were and are a Ramsey," the old man said sadly. "She tried to wipe the existence of your parents from your mind," he accused. "There is much for you to remember. It will take time, but all that has been stolen from you will be restored."

Barbara turned to the Judge, "Who am I legally?"

"Barra Marie Ramsey, by birth," the Judge nodded, adding. "And Barbara Mary Gowan by proxy."

"And everything I've done and accomplished as Barbara Gowan," she frowned, "is that all erased, has that evil woman won?" She turned to glare at the woman who had declared herself the guardian.

"No," the Judge answered with a cryptic smile. "I am going to see that everything is restored to you, Miss Ramsey."

"Miss Ramsey," Barbara repeated. "That's going to take some getting used to. I've used the names Barbara and Gowan so long..." She looked at her grandfather, "Where is my father buried?"

"In our family crypt, in the cemetery in Clark's Town." He answered.

"And my mother?"

Old man Ramsey glared at Marilla, "In a Catholic cemetery, under her maiden name, also in Clark's Town."

"Who gave them the right to do that?" Barbara asked.

The Judge answered, "Mrs. Gowan, as next of kin of the deceased." He was reading off the information from the sheet that Mr. O'Hara had given him.

"I'm the next of kin," Barbara protested. "I wouldn't have done that, buried one, and not the other." She looked at the judge, "Can I sue for exhumation and reburial?"

Amusement filled the Judge's eyes, "You'd be within your rights."

"She has no rights," Mrs. Byrne shouted, "And my family will never allow Mary to be taken from us again." She laughed at Barbara, "You've no means to do such a thing."

"I wouldn't bet on that, Mrs. Byrne." Barbara stood up, "Do not worry, I'll never address you as Aunt, even if your blood does run in my veins." She leaned on the witness stand. "You and your sisters tried to break me, to erase all my memories, and to force me into a life I was never meant to live." Her voice filled with hostility and dark violence, and yet she remained calm. "Your sister, my sainted Grandmother, ordered a doctor to cut my arm off to remove this mark. He rejected her command and told her he'd report her to the authorities. That was something she desperately didn't want."

"You imagined that," Marilla began looking about, "She is raving."

"I was six years old, and my hearing was perfect." Barbara countered. "She didn't even have the decency to come into the room and see me. She stood outside the examining room, with a lawyer who also argued with her. I pretended not to hear, I learned from Sister Mary Joseph what happens when I asked questions they didn't want answered. If you don't believe me ask Mother Angelica." She turned to the Judge, "You say I was unlawfully taken," he nodded. "Who was my legal guardian, my parents never would have left me without protection from them." She pointed at Marilla.

"I was," her grandfather answered. "And you're right, I'd have never allowed one of them near you."

"Can I have her arrested?" Barbara asked.

"There's a list of charges you can press," The Judge leaned back and smiled. "Starting with kidnapping," he said.

Barbara looked at her grandfather, "I cannot be forgiving of this," she said. "I hope you'll understand what I'm about to do."

He studied her face, nodded, and said, "Do what I could not, be the Raven."

Barbara looked again to the Judge, "Who else can I have charged? Who else in that family did this to me?"

Mrs. Byrne glowered at her, "If you charge me, you'll have to charge members of the church as well."

"No," Barbara said, "The late Bishop, perhaps, but the good sisters, except for Sister Mary Joseph, are victims same as me." She looked over at the two Sisters and the Bishop, "You tried to protect me, even from others in your own orders. I will not be vindictive to you. I doubt you knew I wasn't a Roman Catholic up until today."

Mother Angelica sighed, "I should have suspected something was wrong, that woman that dropped you off refused to answer my questions." She hung her head in shame, "I am sorry I failed you, child. We should have been more suspect of the records we received. Had I know you were stolen away; I would have sought out help to return you to your true guardians."

The Bishop stared at Mrs. Byrne, "You've committed crimes against this child and your own church."

"We did what we had to," Mrs. Byrne defended her actions, and those of the rest of her family. "Mary's soul..."

"Mary's soul was happy," the Bishop shouted at her. "She was in love! She was a good woman, and married, and a mother. What her mother did was insane!"

"She was a fallen," Mrs. Byrne glowered. "Her marriage was an abomination, as is that child. Even with a Catholic upraising, she's a hideous sin in the eyes of God."

"I am no such thing," Barbara retorted. "What I am, is someone who has been forced to fit the grove you deemed I should fit. I will not take the veil. It is not my calling."

"God have mercy on you," Mrs. Byrne turned her back on her, "I am done with you."

"You should never have had any say in my life," Barbara responded with heated words that held weight. "You stole me from my bed, you and my Grandmother. You had those officers threaten our housekeeper, you took me away in the dead of night, like thieves. That's what you and your family are, thieves. And likely murderers!" She looked at the Judge, "I want her charged, and I want my mother's body exhumed and returned to my father."

"No," Mrs. Byrne turned around. "You cannot have her; she doesn't belong to you."

"She's my mother! I think I have more say than you, Mrs. Byrne." She continued. "I want to have state officers investigate the circumstances of my parent's accident. I want my mother's remains returned to me, and I want her to rest beside her husband, my father."

"I see you dead first," Mrs. Byrne threatened.

SIGN OF THE RAVEN

"Do your worst." Barbara challenged. "You haven't broken me yet, and as to trying to kill me..." she paused and gave Mrs. Byrne an icy smile. "I'm harder to kill than you think."

Her grandfather smirked and looked over at the woman who for years had said she was Barbara's guardian. "I think ye've met yer match," he said with a slight accent.

The Judge slammed his gavel down, "I'll not have death threats made to anyone in my courtroom," he warned. "Mrs. Byrne, you and your family are in serious trouble."

She turned her glare on the Judge, "You thought I was trouble ten years ago. You have no idea of the trouble you've brought down on yourself now. If you side with is misbegotten devil's spawn, I can guarantee that you will not only lose your appointment, but everything you have!"

The Judge made another note, "Keep going Marilla," he muttered.

"I'll see to it, that you won't even get elected dog catcher," she shouted. "Now have these cuffs taken off my wrists and arrest that bitch for impersonating a Gowan!"

The Judge tossed his pen down, leaned back and laughed coldly. "Marilla, all these years, and I thought you didn't have a sense of humor."

"Stop laughing you fool," she screamed. "I'm serious. Arrest her!"

"Sorry, Marilla, no can do." The Judge said. "The witnesses here have all said that the girl known as Barbara Gowan acted in good faith in using that name. If anyone is guilty of fraud, it's you, and the late Mrs. Gowan." The Judge shook his head, "I suppose I should subpoena her surviving son as well, why not get the whole family down here."

Mrs. Byrne glared, "I want my lawyer," she glowered. "You can't stop me from seeing my lawyer."

"You can see him as soon as the charges have been made," the Judge decreed, "and not an instant sooner."

"This is a travesty!"

"I agree," the Judge nodded, "what you and your cohorts have done is a travesty of justice. Justice may be blind, but I am not! It may take me time, but I'll find the local officers you used, and they too will join in being arrested and paying for what was done to this child."

"Your Honor," a man in a dark suit entered the courtroom, "I represent Mrs. Byrne!" He was older, distinguished, and commanding. "I demand to know why my client has been dragged into court."

Mr. O'Hara, who'd been silently enjoying the spectacle before him, stood up and addressed him. "Good morning, Uriah, I've waited a long time for this moment."

"Morton, get me out of here," Mrs. Byrne demanded.

Uriah Morton looked past her, to the young woman on the stand. "I pray to God; this isn't what I think it is."

"OH, Uriah, you've missed all the fun." Mr. O'Hara passed him a copy of the original complaint, and the notes he'd made since coming into the court. "Put your glasses on, Uriah," Mr. O'Hara suggested. "You're going to need them."

He read the first paragraph and made a quiet little moan sound. He read the second and lowered the paper to look at Barbara on the stand, still standing and her grandfather standing next to her. He read on and then began to read the notes. He looked at the Bishop, inclined his head and read on. He looked at the two nuns, and let a heavy sigh go. He then read something that made him look uncomfortable.

Uriah lowered the pages, "I had nothing to do with Mrs. Kathrine Gowan," he said. "I have no prior knowledge of what she did, or whom she had working for her." He was addressing the Judge. "Has my client been charged?"

"We're working on it." The Judge said.

Mrs. Byrne glared, "I said have me uncuffed!"

"Be still," Uriah ordered. "You're in trouble, and I'm going to do my best to get you free, but you must be still."

"Get her free?" Barbara spoke up, "You mean to get her off? Have you any idea of what she's done?" She left the witness stand. "What she and her sisters did to me? Or the insult done my father?"

Uriah didn't look pleased at being addressed in this manner. "See here young woman," he began.

"No," Barbara spoke with force and he took a step back. "You see here!" she pointed a finger at him. "If you're her lawyer, you're aware that she's been masquerading as my guardian. That she's had me locked up in a convent school, without benefit of outlet. She had me socially isolated! That she's been pushing for me to take the veil, that she had to be forced by the Bishop to allow me to accept a scholarship that I was awarded after years of hard work... that she has now had that scholarship pulled and that she is accusing me of fraud."

Uriah turned to Mrs. Byrne. "Marilla!"

"That she had me locked out of my dorm room and that she has stolen my belongings." Barbara accused. "And you're going to get her off?" her voice dripped sarcasm. "I don't think so!"

"You can't believe a word that comes out of that creature's mouth," Marilla said. "We should have placed her in an asylum. She's a compulsive liar. I know Doctors who will back me up!"

"Mrs. Byrne," the Bishop moved out of his seat, "do not dare to defame that child any more than you have! Your soul, yours madam, is in jeopardy. Not hers!"

"What have I lied about?" Barbara demanded, still walking toward Marilla Byrne. "Name one thing?" She heard the anger, but for once in her life, did nothing to quell it. "Did your sister, my own Grandmother, not have me dragged from my bed? Despite the efforts of my parent's housekeeper to keep the so-called officials from taking me? Did she not have me delivered to a Convent school in the dead of night? Did she not leave me there, and never come to see me, to even check on my circumstances? Did she not prevent me from being at my parent's funerals?"

"You were a child," Mrs. Byrne said with disdain, "children have no business being at a funeral."

"I was never allowed so much as a picture of my parents to remember them by," Barbara's argument was passionate. "No contact from any family member on either side."

Dane Ramsey chimed in, "Mrs. Gowan had not right to take Barra out of her home, I was legal guardian, not she!"

Mrs. Byrne ignored him and addressed Barbara who was still moving toward her, "Your grandmother tried to save your soul, and the thanks we get is you bringing unfounded charges up against me?"

"Don't try to turn this around," Barbara said, "I am the victim here, not you, old woman! You and your family have done nothing but try and break me! You've kept me from family that would have nurtured me!"

"WE gave you a good Catholic upbringing!" Mrs. Byrne defended the actions taken on Barbara's behalf. "You were raised in a manner that would save your soul."

"I was isolated," Barbara now stood within feet of her foe. "I was treated like a leaper, a disease, a creature of scorn. I was never given an ounce of understanding. Sister Mary Joseph slapped me so hard, she rendered me unconscious! You think that is to save my soul? She could have killed me... and what would you have done? Buried me in a pauper's grave?"

Mrs. Byrne turned to her lawyer, "Must I be harassed in this manner by this creature?"

"I'd say, you've earned it," the lawyer muttered.

"Never once was I allowed to come 'home' for vacation or break," Barbara reminded the woman who had usurped the place of her rightful guardian. "I was only allowed to learn, not play, not even learn to play music."

"You were supposed to become useful," Mrs. Byrne argued. "Not be pampered."

SIGN OF THE RAVEN

"Pampered?" Barbara challenged. "You refused me a decent wardrobe for coming to the college, how is that pampered? I came here in rags from the poor box."

Mrs. Byrne glared at her, "You're not dressed in rags now."

"No, I paid for these things from thrift stores from the meager allowance the Bishop insisted on and learned to use my friend's mother's sewing machine!" Barbara retorted. "I earned money to pay for other things by tutoring other students! None of this came from you, not even the laptop that you confiscated from my dorm room!"

"I hardly think that you are capable of earning that much money," Mrs. Byrne stated. "The reports on you were that you were not that smart, I still cannot fathom how you managed to get that scholarship!" She glared at Barbara with hatred in her eyes, "You must have cheated. If I can prove it, I will."

"Mrs. Byrne," Mother Mary Clare stood up, taking umbrage with the statement. "We are strict when issuing the tests that are taken by our students. Miss Gowan,..."

"She is not a Gowan, do not call her by that name," Mrs. Byrne complained.

"That is the name *your sister* registered her by," Mother Mary Clare responded. "That is the name on our records. She was a fine student, even though you wanted us to restrict her ability to compete in classes. I don't know who told you she wasn't bright, for it wasn't any of us. It was you who said she shouldn't learn to use a computer, but it was the Bishop who insisted that she be taught. While other students were free to use their computer lab time for frivolous pursuits Barbara was only allowed access to limited programs. She learned to manage her time, and to study harder than any other girl. She should have graduated at the top of her class! She should have been the class Valedictorian. You refused to allow her even that honor."

"She does not deserve any of that," Mrs. Byrne shouted at the startled nun. "She is an abomination in the eyes of God!"

"I beg to differ with you," the Bishop harshly interjected. "She is a good and generous person, despite your treatment of her. She is helpful and giving and is not an abomination." He looked at Barbara, "I have no idea who pulled your scholarship, for it wasn't me! As far as the church is concerned, you earned that scholarship."

"She was conceived in sin!" Mrs. Byrne argued. "Her mother didn't have our permission to run off and marry that devil."

"Mary Gowan was twenty-one years old," Mr. O'Hara said. "She was of legal age of consent in this state, she didn't need permission."

"How can you call yourself a good Catholic?" Mrs. Byrne demanded. "That girl should have listened to her parents. If she had, she'd still be alive. She disobeyed her father and her mother. They told her to have nothing to do with that devil, Roan Ramsey."

"My son was not a devil." Dane Ramsey said. "Granted he was high spirited, but from the moment Mary walked into his life, until he drew his last breath, he was a changed man."

Barbara glared at Mrs. Byrne. "You showed me no mercy, and that is what I will have for you. No mercy." She looked at the Judge. "I'm ready to sign that complaint."

"I'll counter sign," the Bishop offered.

"I'll witness," said Mother Angelica and Mary Clare together.

Chapter 8.

Mr. O'Hara, and Mrs. Byrne's lawyer were taken into the Judge's chambers. Mrs. Byrne distanced herself from the Bishop and the two nuns. Barbara took a seat beside her grandfather Ramsey and Trey.

"Are you sure you know what you've done?" Dane Ramsey inquired. "It's a hornet's nest you've poked."

"She knows," Trey said supportively. "She knows what it is she has to do. Barra has been planning this for an exceedingly long time."

"Exhumation is going to be tricky," Dane warned. "That family has played fast and loose with the rules, they don't like being called on it. Mrs. Byrne wasn't kidding when she said her family had power."

"I believe they murdered my parents, and had plans to murder me, but that nun Sister Mary Joseph was caught." Barbara whispered. "They really see me as a threat."

"They tried to steal your inheritance as well as your life," Dane cautioned. "That lawyer may not have been in on it, he wasn't Mrs. Gowan's man, that's true. However, Mrs. Gowan's lawyers tried to steal everything that by law goes to you."

"I want the name of the Gowan lawyer," Barbara murmured darkly. "This Raven wants it all back."

"Revenge won't bring your father or your mother back," Dane said, putting a comforting arm about her shoulders. "Nor will it give you peace."

"I'm not going for revenge, I'm demanding justice. It may stop them," Barbara said. "I want to know every name that was in on this crime."

Dane frowned, "You don't think they are going to stop. You think they are going to..."

"Try and kill me," she finished for him. "Yes."

"Why on earth?"

"Grandfather," she looked at him, "They are not living in any type of reality. They think the church had the right to cloister me, and to keep me prisoner. They think they had the right to murder my mother and my father. They have lived with this secret for nearly sixteen years, and she doesn't think she or they did anything wrong. They wanted me erased."

Trey agreed with Barbara, "They are now trying to erase her from the rolls in the College, and to destroy her academic life. To make what she achieved nonexistent."

"That woman thinks she has power," Barbara reminded her grandfather. "She threatened the Judge... and she has no remorse in having done so. She's not going to confide in her lawyer, he's but a dupe to get her free. There's someone beyond him, someone higher up in this family. Mr. Morgan said Old man Gowan had power... he must have passed his gauntlet to someone."

"Why would you say that?"

"History," Trey and Barbara said together.

Dane looked over at Marilla Byrne, "She's not afraid," he observed. "She is up to something."

"I wonder who called her lawyer," Barbara whispered. "I wish I could talk to the arresting officer right now."

"That wouldn't do you any good," Trey warned. "But trust your instincts," he whispered, "like you would in the game."

She nodded, "I was thinking that myself." She looked past Mrs. Byrne to the president of the College, and the Bursar. "That's a nervous pair if ever I saw one."

"You may have to sue them," Trey acknowledged. "They know it. They screwed up, and they know that too."

"I don't like having to take down the President of the school, because the Bursar did something stupid." Barbara muttered. "At least we know the Bishop didn't have the scholarship pulled."

"No mercy was shown you," Trey reminded her. "Do not show them your soft side. Keep that for family, the family you choose, the one you make."

She nodded, "I remember." She told him.

"Good." Trey turned toward the door the two lawyers and the Judge had entered. "This may not end here," he warned. "We may have to fight all the way to the state supreme court."

"I'm ready," she whispered.

Trey looked at her, and smirked, "You didn't go and backup all those files you've been compiling, did you?"

"Original and copies," she said. "And I have put them in a safe place. I put them in a safe place before Solstice."

"You're far smarter than that family knew," Trey praised.

"Let us hope, it's smart enough," Barbara suggested.

The door to the Judge's chamber opened, and Mr. O'Hara exited, he motioned for Barbara to come to where he stood. When she was within feet of him, he said. "The Judge wishes to speak to you."

Barbara nodded, and followed him into the chambers. She took a seat and prepared for a fight. "You wished to speak to me?"

"Mr. Morton here wishes to offer you a… deal." The Judge said.

Barbara sighed, took a deep breath and turned to him, "Before you begin, Mr. Morton, I want you to consider the people you are working for. No matter what you offer me, Mrs. Byrne is going to balk."

Morton scratched his chin, "That she may," he agreed. "But it's my job to try and lessen any damages."

"Even if she's the one who created them currently?" Barbara asked.

"Yes." He nodded.

"What is your offer?" She asked.

"I will have her drop her charges and end this foolish vendetta and have your scholarship restored. In return you will drop your charges against your Great Aunt and will cease trying to cause problems about your mother's internment."

"No," Barbara said softly, shaking her head.

"I'm offering you your education, that you've worked so hard for, your degrees. Your future." He said, trying to reason with her. "Are they not worth the price of peace?"

"No," She stood up, and faced him. "My Grandmother and her sisters barred me from attending my mother's funeral. They have kept the place of her burial secret from me, not allowing me to even visit. They kept my very name from me. What you offer is nothing. They will not keep your terms, and I think you know it. But they will expect me to keep my word, because I am honorable. No, Mr. Morton, I will not agree to your terms, and you'd best thank God I don't." She looked at the Judge, "I will sign that complaint now."

The Judge stared at Morton, "I told you she wasn't foolish!" He passed a paper across his desk. "I suggest you sign both your real name and the one you've lived under. That way they can't claim fraud."

"I had planned on using both." She signed the paper. "I'm sorry Mr. Morton, I know you're only doing your job. But I should warn you, whoever is pulling the strings, and I know it's not Marilla Byrne, but whoever they are... They are not going to be happy with you for even suggesting this offer. I'd watch my back if I were you."

"I've a feeling you're right," Morton said. He looked at the Judge, "Will they arraign her here?"

"Yes, this afternoon."

BARBARA SAT IN THE nearly empty courtroom with Mr. O'Hara. "I want to be here," she said. "The other shoe is about to drop, and I don't want to miss it."

"I think you should be here," O'Hara said. "We've located the service that was allowed into your dorm room, and they have been subpoenaed. They have also been issued a cease and desist order."

"And my belongings?"

"Are in lockup," he said. "Once all the formality is done, they will be returned, and the company will compensate you."

"Compensate," Barbara understood, something had been damaged. "I am still out of the dorm," Barbara murmured. "And my classes."

"You could stay with us," he offered. "You know you are always welcome."

"No, not making a target out of your family," Barbara said. "The Byrne family and the Gowan have blood on their hands now, I won't tempt them to make things worse." She shook her head, "How many others have been party to this conspiracy? There were two other sisters, two other guardians." Barbara looked at Mr. O'Hara. "No, I can't come to your house, I cannot put your family in danger."

"I have a friend who runs a rooming house," he suggested. "Nice widow woman, usually rents to visiting professors."

"I'll have to think about that one," she said. "The college still hasn't agreed to fix the mess with the scholarship. I'm suspended, I don't have classes. I doubt they would even allow me on campus to audit."

"You could go stay with Dane Ramsey," O'Hara said. "He'd like to get to know you, don't you want to know him?"

"I do want to get to know him," Barbara confessed. "But not like this. It's not fair to him, to toss me at him and say, take her in, she's yours."

"You don't trust him?"

"I don't trust circumstances," she said. "Too easy to cover things over and forget me. As it is, the college doesn't want to accept responsibility for having tossed me out. Mrs. Byrne doesn't want to accept that she and my grandmother and their other sisters pulled a fraud on the church and everyone else. Going off to live with Grandfather Ramsey would let them all off the hook. They all want to forget me, forget what they did to me."

"I won't let them," O'Hara vowed.

"The crimes committed against me, and my parents, go deep, Mr. O'Hara. Whoever is the top player in this game is dangerous," she warned. "This is a long shot from being over. I need to stay here and stay visible."

"You don't think that Mrs. Byrne is the ringleader, so to speak." O'Hara mused.

"No," Barbara warned. "This is complex, it's like a war game. Oh, I believe that she and my grandmother were high up in the plotting of this. God knows, they are batshit crazy. But I don't think they were at the top." She frowned, "The Bursar froze my student accounts," she complained. "What cash I have isn't enough to make it through what could be a long court case."

The Bishop, who'd been sitting behind them since the court emptied, spoke quietly. "The church has a responsibility here," he said softly. "We failed you, and to allow you to just be tossed into the street is not something I can live with. I could arrange for you to room in the convent here, while things are made straight."

Barbara gave him a quizzical look, decided he was on the level, before she spoke, "I thank you, your Eminence, I do. However, I've had my fill of Convents."

The Bishop shook his head, sadly, "You haven't had the best of experiences with the Church, have you?"

"No," Barbara said. "I have not," she agreed.

"I didn't know my predecessor," the Bishop said. "Oh, I'd met him on rare occasions, but I didn't *know* him. We were not friendly or even remotely close." He crossed his arms, "I cannot for the life of me fathom how he got roped into this... conspiracy."

"If I had to make a bet," Barbara said lightly, "I'd say he had some personal connection to the Gowan family." She offered the Bishop a half-hearted smile. "I don't blame you; you've been wonderful since you took your oath of station. Being Bishop must be exceedingly difficult. Having to deal with a family feud is not what you signed up for."

"No," the Bishop agreed. "It's not."

"Barbara," Mr. O'Hara said, "I am not going to just let you walk the streets. You need a safe place to stay."

"I think I can offer that," Trey said.

"I'm not sending her home with you," Mr. O'Hara said grimly. "She has a reputation that needs to be protected."

"I wasn't suggesting anything inappropriate." Trey teased. "Mr. Morgan, who is living in my guest cottage has offered his spare bedroom." He smiled broadly, "He's nearly eighty, has a full-time live-in nurse, and a housekeeper, and is most respected in the community."

"That's kind of him," Barbara said.

"Barra," Trey took a seat, "It's safe and it's secure. More important, it's close. No one is going to forget you."

"Does he have any idea of what he could be letting himself in for?" She asked. "They want me dead, Trey!"

"Morgan remembers your parents," Trey countered. "He said he'd take on the Gowan's with one arm tied behind his back."

O'Hara laughed, "He could too. You don't know his history. He went up against Old Man Gowan once, and Gowan went off licking his wounds."

"I don't want anyone else hurt," Barbara said standing up. "It's bad enough I don't know which name to answer to." She began to pace the open aisle. "I've lived all this time as Barbara, now I learn my given name is Barra...." She shook her head, "Neither name feels like it is my own just yet."

"If you had to choose," Trey said, "What name would you answer to?"

She gave it a moment's consideration, was on the verge of answering when Warren and Dawn entered, and he called out, "Barb!" He and Dawn moved up the aisle, and he looked fit to be tied, "What's this shit I hear, you've been kicked out? And that you've been arrested?"

She turned to Trey, "Barb, it's a bit of both and neither." She then addressed Warren. "Warren, don't get involved."

"Too late," Dawn said. "He formed a petition drive the moment he heard that the Bursar kicked you out of the dorm." Her thumb moved in the direction of her young man. "When he heard they pulled your scholarship and suspended your degrees, he went apeshit."

Warren nodded, a proud grin on his face, "I left the office, and went to the college and protested the injustice."

"Warren," Barbara placed a hand to her face, "You left work?"

"My father left with me," he announced, "Said that if it weren't for you, I'd have never passed my classes. He's right, you were the best tutor we ever hired."

"But Warren," Barbara argued. "This is not your fight."

"Yes, it is," he countered. "For four years you've worked like a demon to get your studies done and help the rest of us all the while carrying a full class load; who cares what name you go by?"

"They've released that information?" Barbara wasn't happy, how dare they? "The smear campaign has started?"

"The college is trying to cover their own ass," Warren complained. "The fact that you're an asset doesn't seem to matter to them." He suddenly noticed the Bishop sitting there, "Sir," he acknowledged him. "Sorry about the language."

"I'm impressed by the friends you've made," the Bishop said. "After years of isolation and being made to sit things out."

"What's he talking about?" Warren asked.

"I was raised in convent schools since I was five," Barbara answered.

"No shit?" Warren said, then shrugged at the cleric. "Sorry." He looked back at Barbara, "Is that way you dressed so weird those first few months here?"

She nodded, "My clothes came out of the poor-box." She looked down at the dated outfit she was wearing, "And now out of thrift stores."

SIGN OF THE RAVEN

"Nothing wrong with thrift," Warren said. "Some of my happiest memories are thrifting with my mom." He leaned toward her, "You don't get rich and stay rich if you go around spending like a demon."

Trey smiled at Barbara, "Some of his early costuming choices came from a thrift store."

"Until I learned other means of getting my supplies," Warren agreed. "Then I got all head swelled, and you took care of that by knocking some sense back into me when you knocked me on my ass." He smiled broadly, "My father says you reminded me of what the purpose of the Conquest game is all about. Building a civilization, and maintaining it. He wasn't happy about it at first, but he saw you were the real deal."

"You made him a better boyfriend," Dawn said. "He's so thoughtful now." She showed off her engagement ring. "And he'll be a wonderful husband." She tucked her arm into Warren's. "We'd have broken up if not for you."

"I won't take credit for that," Barbara protested. "I will say, I enjoyed knocking him on his ass, twice."

"And with a prop, no less," Warren laughed. "But making me play dead actually was good." He shrugged, "Who knew all I needed was a reality check?"

"I did," Trey said. "But I was glad it was Bar...Barb who gave it to you." He tried the name and liked it. He moved closer, "Life in this valley would not be the same, if not for you."

"Trey," she blushed. "You don't know that."

"I know that you've changed all of us," he said, taking her hand into his. "I know that my life would be dull as tears, and I might not have made the move to buy the orchard if it had not been for you coming into our lives."

"I disagree," she countered, "you'd have bought the orchard. You might not have been so gun-ho to fix the house..."

"I want it to be our home..."

161

Warren whistled, "Are you two an item now?"

"Yes," Trey said.

"No," Barbara said at the same time. Then frowned, "I don't know, maybe."

"There is no maybe about it," Trey lifted the Thor's hammer she wore. "She's my girl, she just hasn't accepted that its fate!"

"See," Warren said, "You are the fixed point that we all revolve around."

Mr. O'Hara nodded, "They are never going to be able to sweep you under the carpet."

"I'm even working on a sit in until they put you back in classes," Warren warned.

"Your father won't like that," Barbara groaned.

"It was his idea," Warren said wryly.

Barbara stared, confused for a moment, "Really? I didn't think he liked me."

"Well, not at first," Warren admitted. "But then you did smack me down and take my stuff... was he supposed to be thrilled?"

"He's lucky Mr. O'Hara didn't sue you for injuring Caitlyn." Barbara reminded him.

"Yes, and once he saw the tape of what I had done, he read me the riot act and told me that if I didn't shape up, he was going to let you beat the crap out of me on a daily basis." Warren said.

Everyone but Barbara burst out laughing, "It was serious Warren," she said.

"Barb," Trey said the name again, lightly, and looked at her. "It suits you." He changed the subject. "So, Barb, when we are done here today, I'll drive you out to the Morgan Orchard and the cottage. You can make plans on your strategy from there. We'll make arrangements for a car and driver to be at your disposal."

Barbara weighed her options, "It does seem the best solution to my current state of affairs."

"Mr. Morgan isn't easily intimidated," Trey said. "He liked your father and wasn't happy with the way the investigation into the accident got sidelined."

O'Hara picked up the conversation, "I've already ordered copies of the accident records and the reports, and I've started looking into it." He assured Barbara. "There's some long-time law officials locally who are not going to be happy."

"Can we do something about a fifteen, sixteen-year-old incident?" She asked. "Haven't the statues of limitations kicked in?"

"Not on murder," O'Hara said darkly. "And if my instincts are right, and the witnesses whose statements were never used are correct, your parents were murdered."

"Does my grandfather know?" she asked, worried about how this was going to affect him.

"I've talked to him, warned him more to the point." Mr. O'Hara stated firmly. "Because of whom you are, and the mountain of evidence we have with you, he said to do what must be done. He supports your efforts to find justice."

"That is what I want," she nodded. "I thought it was revenge, but the more I think about it, I want justice." She looked at everyone gathered around her to give her support. "My parents deserve justice." She was grateful that the scholarship had landed her here, in Danbury so close to Clark's Town. She was thankful that she had risen above the abuse and the isolation that her Grandmother had placed her in. That Mrs. Byrne had not been successful in forcing her to take vows she could never honor. "I'd be honored if all of you here, right now, would stay to see this through with me."

Warren moved forward, "You are my Clan leader," he said in the voice he used in the game. "I would never let you face this alone. As your Steward, it is my duty to stand with you."

"You rescued me from the castle," Dawn said moving to his side, "Gave me your name and banner, it is my honor to stand with you."

"You are the woman I love," Trey said standing also. "I would face the fires of hell at your side."

The Bishop stood, "The church failed you up to now, I won't allow it to go further."

The two Sisters of Hope stood up as well, "We'd like to make amends, and stand for you now, when we should have years ago." Mother Angelica stated.

Mr. O'Hara stood, "You are my extended family, and have been since the day that Caitlyn brought you home. It will be an honor to stand at your side."

Barbara looked at them, tears shinning in her dark eyes, "I couldn't be prouder to be in any other company," she said.

MR. O'HARA SAT BESIDE Barbara as the courtroom began to fill. Behind them sat the Bishop, Trey, Warren, and Dawn and the two Mother Superiors. Grandfather Ramsey had returned to the courtroom and sat on the other side of Barbara with a concerned expression on his face.

"Marilla Byrne is up to something," Grandfather Ramsey commented. "Look at that haughty smirk on her face."

Mr. O'Hara casually glanced over, "Yes," he nodded, "she thinks she's one upped us."

Barbara didn't bother to look, "You did something she doesn't know about," she whispered. O'Hara nodded. "Did you ever play checkers?"

"No," O'Hara snickered, "I play chess." He turned and looked at his daughter's friend. "Have from the time I was ten," he confided.

"She thinks she's smarter," Barbara warned.

"She's about to learn she's not as smart as she thinks," O'Hara assured.

SIGN OF THE RAVEN

"Hear ye, hear ye," the bailiff called out. "The court of Danbury in the county of Essex is about to convene."

Mr. Morton looked nervous, he looked at the door leading to the Judge's chambers. His hands fidgeted, and he looked ready to jump out of his skin. He looked down at the legal document in his hands and didn't see when the door opened. He only heard the bailiff call everyone to stand.

"Your honor," he said without looking up, "I have a request for you to recuse yourself...." At that moment he looked up. "You're not Judge MacAfee!"

The man seated behind the bench gave him a cold, icy stare. "No, I'm not. I'm Federal Judge Bankert," he hit the gavel on the little wooden block. "This court will come to order." He looked at Morton. "Judge MacAfee felt that as there were more charges here that were of a state and federal issue, that he should turn this portion over to me."

Morton stood, lips quivering and words spilling out, but nothing that was audible. He turned to his client.

Marilla glared, "Who the hell are you?"

"Someone who doesn't like being insulted, madam." The Judge warned. "Just what was the reason you wanted the Judge to recuse himself?"

Morton babbled. "His involvement with too many of the principals in this case...."

Bankert frowned, "He was worried you'd pull something like this," he warned. "If there are no other objections..."

There was a commotion at the back of the courtroom. A tall man with graying temples and dark wavy hair entered. Followed by what looked to be a team of lawyers. Marilla smiled like a cat that had eaten a cage full of canaries. The Judge hit his gavel and shouted, "I will have quite and order!"

The man who entered, dressed in an expensive business suit came forward, apolitically. "Your Honor forgive this intrusion. I've only just learned that my Aunt was brought here..."

"And who are you?" The Judge asked.

"I'm Marshall Gowan, Marilla Byrne is the sister of my late mother." He said. "I am the head of the family, not that you would know it by the behavior of my relations."

Barbara leaned to look him over. He was not nearly as sinister in appearance as his aunt. He had removed his overcoat, and laid it on a chair, he looked upset with Marilla. He placed a finger to his lips, silencing her, and took a seat at her table, his lawyers replaced the mousy little Mr. Morton.

Judge Bankert looked suddenly amused. "If we are all assembled," He looked at the Gowan table, not at Barbara. "The charges being brought against your Aunt here are very serious."

Marshall Gowan turned and looked at her, "I was under the impression that she was bringing charges against a person for impersonating a member of my family."

"No."

Marshall looked at the Judge, "May I ask what the charges are?"

"First charge is aiding and abetting the kidnapping of one Barra Marie Ramsey," the Judge said.

"That's not possible," Marshall said. "That child is dead."

"No, I am not," Barbara said standing up.

Marshall stared at Barbara. His mouth opened, but no words came out.

"The second charge is helping in falsifying a birth certificate and aiding in the forcibly taking custody of Miss Ramsey, on the night of her parent's accident." The Judge said.

"My sister's child died," Marshall said, still staring at Barbara. "Shortly after my sister."

"Third charge is aiding and abetting the murder of Mr. Roan Ramsey and his wife Mary Gowan Ramsey." The Judge read, looked over the top of the document at Marilla.

"It's a lie," Marilla shouted, "you cannot believe a single word that liar says."

Marshall stared, first at his aunt, then at the Judge, lastly at Barbara. "Murder?" He shook his head, "I knew the family was angry, that my father had been most vocal about not liking Mary being married to Roan... But Murder?" He grew red in the face, and Barbara worried he was going to turn violent on her. Instead, he spun on his team of lawyers. "Which of you little snakes were part of my father's and my mother's law team?"

Three hands went up.

"Is this true? Was I lied to overseas, so I wouldn't come home and stop them?" He accused. "Did my mother steal my sister's child? Did my mother kill my sister and her husband? And why was I told my sister's child died?"

"Mr. Gowan," one of the lawyers tried to sooth him. "It's not what you are thinking..."

"My sister told me before I went overseas that she and Roan had arranged for Dane Ramsey to be little Barra's guardian should anything happen to them!" he shouted. "Then my mother wire's me that Roan and Mary were killed in an accident and that the baby died of influenza!" He slammed his hand on the table. "Someone had better tell me the truth and fast." He glared at his aunt, "What did you do, you hideous old woman? What in the living Hell did you and my mother do?"

Marilla looked stunned, "Marshall, I will not tolerate that tone."

"Oh, you'll do more than that," he threatened. "You will tell me the truth, or I'll ask this nice Bishop to excommunicate your sorry ass right now!"

"You can't," she wailed. "We were trying to save Mary's soul... don't you see?"

"No, I don't see." He shouted. "You let me think Mary's child was dead all this time. That Ramsey wouldn't allow us to even go to its funeral and had it buried in secret. That he had buried his son, and left Mary in the morgue! Was that a lie too, Aunt Marilla?"

"I never meant for you to suffer.... Your brother Michael agreed with us..." She fretted. "So, did James.... If they were still alive, you'd never have to learn of this..." She looked past him and glared at Barbara. "Had that bitch taken the veil as we planned none of this would be happening."

Marshall turned away from his aunt, disgusted. He moved over to the table where Barbara was still standing. "She was a baby the last time I saw her," he murmured. He pointed to her arm, "My sister's child had a brand..." Barbara pulled up her sleeve. "It's true... you're my sister's child." He looked at her, Marshall Gowan whispered, "You have your father's eyes."

"I don't know you," she whispered. "They forced me to live under an assumed name. They raised me a Catholic, even though I wasn't baptized one. I don't know you." She stepped back. "I'm not sure I can even trust you. You are one of them..."

"No, Barra, I'm not one of them! I was your mother's youngest brother," he said. "I knew about Mary and Roan; I even came to your house a few times. I had hoped that everyone would cool down. But when my father died, my mother chased your mom and dad out of the funeral home... with you.... I saw that it was hopeless. Had I known what my mother and brothers and aunts and God knows who else, were capable of, I wouldn't have gone to Dublin to learn the banking system." He looked at the Judge, "As far as I'm concerned, you can throw the book at Marilla Byrne and these three," he pointed to the lawyers who had worked for his mother. "I will agree to any restitution that the court decrees."

"Marshall, no!" Marilla screamed. "WE can win this; we can force her back into the convent and your sister's soul will be at rest."

"My sister's soul will never be at rest as long as you torment her child!" He countered. "I cannot sanction what you've done. No sane man would!"

"Mr. Gowan," Barbara addressed him carefully, "She and your mother, and their sisters may well have been guilty of murder."

He glared at the three lawyers who were looking guiltier than Marilla. "If you had anything to do with the murder of my sister," he glowered, "I will see you in hell." He looked at his Aunt. "Killing her and her husband is not saving her soul, it has damned your own."

Marilla stared at him, as if he'd lost his mind. "You cannot be serious. You know that Roan was the devil incarnate!"

"I know only that Roan Ramsey loved my sister, that he was willing to convert if she wished it." Marshall stated. He looked at the Judge, "I came here this afternoon, under the impression that my Aunt was being wrongfully accused. I stand here now and state, that no more Gowan funds will be used to continue this vendetta. If she and these men who worked for my father and later my mother, are guilty of having a hand in the death of my sister and her husband, let them rot." He said. Then addressed the lawyers who hadn't raised their hands, "Should I discover that you had anything to do with this… you'd best pray to God for mercy, you won't find any from me."

The Judge leaned on his bench, "I am going to place bail high; I find you all to be flight risks," he said with amusement. "Bail is set at three million apiece."

Mrs. Byrne shoved the lawyer out of her way, "I want my son… he'll see that this ends here and now."

Marshall stared at his aunt, "Robert called me this morning, he had to leave town." He turned to the Judge, "I have a feeling you'll have to send out officers to arrest him. He never liked Roan; he was thick as thieves with my older brothers. Up until this morning, he held a high-ranking position in my family's business... he was placed there by my father. If I know my cousin, he's going to get out of the country as quick as he can."

DANE HAD BEEN SILENT, and Barbara turned to him when they took Marilla away in handcuffs. "Grandfather, this is only the beginning. Things will not end here."

"I know," he looked at Trey, "Lochwood tells me you're going to stay with Mr. Morgan over at the orchard. You know you have a house of your own," he said. "I kept the house in Clark's Town."

Barbara shook her head, "I can't go there," she said. "I apricate that you kept it, but... I can't go there; I still have nightmares about the night I was taken from my bed."

"I understand," he said. "With your permission, I'll have it cleared out and sold."

"I think that's best, I can't live in that house." She paused. "Grandfather, were there any picture albums?"

Dane nodded, "I kept all of the albums that Mary started. I'll have them delivered to you at the orchard." He stood up, "May I come to call on you?"

"I'd like that," she said. "I have no idea of what will happen next."

Marshall Gowan cleared his throat, "I'm going to do what I can to overturn the trouble Marilla caused you. I'm going to see if we can't get that scholarship reinstated and your degrees honored."

"That's kind of you Mr. Gowan." She said coolly.

"I know you don't trust me," he said. "But I swear to God, I had nothing to do with this hideous plot to destroy your family." He kept his distance, knowing that she was skittish. "I hope in time, you'll come to call me uncle, or at least by my name." He nodded to them and turned to leave with his team of remaining lawyers.

"He's not a bad man, Barra." Dane said softly. "Give him a chance to prove himself to you; Roan liked Marshall."

"I will take your suggestion under advisement," she said. "I will make no promise at this time, Grandfather." She looked about the courtroom. "I wonder if I will ever feel that I've gotten justice. All I feel right now is that I am once more a pauper."

"A pauper?" her grandfather questioned.

"I'm depending on charity," she whispered. "Just as I had to when I came here." She didn't like the sound of self-pity.

"Barra," her grandfather placed a consoling arm over her shoulder. "You have unlimited funds at your command. Your father left you a very wealthy young woman. Ramsey Fine Cabinets and Tables is still making furniture from your father's designs. I put everything that was your father's share of the profits into trust for you. You don't have to take charity from anyone."

She stared at him, "What are you talking about?"

"One of the things the Gowan lawyers tried to do, was to take control of your estate. But since they didn't have the legal rights to you in the first place, they couldn't touch your inheritance." He explained.

"I was under the impression that I had nothing to my name." Barbara confessed. "The sisters told me I should be grateful for what my guardian was doing for me. That I shouldn't want for more than I was being given." She was trying to comprehend. "You mean I have an inheritance?"

"Kathrine Gowan denied that she'd taken you," her grandfather said, "but the housekeeper had kept a copy of the papers demanding that you be turned over to the officers who came to the house. She then called me; our lawyers sent guards to protect the house. They were there when men came to ransack the house, likely to look for legal papers and whatever they could take that was worth anything. We had state officers, and the thugs dressed as cops decided it wasn't worth going to prison. They weren't even real police officers, just costumed thugs. It took me nearly twenty-four hours to locate my son's remains." He took a seat again. "The Gowan family had him labeled a John Doe."

"But the accident, there was a report," Barbara murmured.

Dane nodded, "There is much about the accident, and the report that to this day, I don't understand. When I asked about Mary, I was told to mind my own business, she'd been collected by *her family*." He shook his head, "She was my daughter in law, and I adored her."

"Is there room where my father is, for her to be at his side?" Barbara asked.

"There is," he assured her. "And you don't have to worry about the cost, I'll cover all the expenses, as I would have had the Gowan's not interfered."

Barbara looked up to see the Judge and Mr. O'Hara coming their way.

"Young lady," the Judge addressed her. "I have the complaints, and the warrants ready to go. A federal investigation is going to be done, this crime was done on a state road, they are Federally funded."

"I apricate your help," she said. "It's been sixteen years, is it possible to find evidence now?"

"Not only evidence, but witnesses," O'Hara assured. "Your Grandmother may have bought the local judge, but she and her family cannot buy the whole government!"

"Then justice will be served." She whispered and closed her eyes. "And my parents will at long last be at peace." She looked at her grandfather, "You said they tried to take control of my inheritance, who was going to oversee it?"

"Robert Byrne," Dane said. "He's a financial lawyer."

Barbara looked at Mr. O'Hara, "I'll bet he's the one pulling the strings. No wonder he's on the run." She looked at Marshal, "Your cousin would let his mother take the fall, wouldn't he?"

Marshal Gowan shrugged, "I wouldn't put it past him."

CHAPTER 9.

Barra Marie Ramsey sat with the O'Hara family, watching Caitlyn advance to the stage to accept her diploma and her degree cords. Her own degrees were still in question, her education effectively halted. The College President would have preferred that she'd not shown up today, but she didn't care about saving his face. She cared about Caitlyn. Trey sat beside her, and Tim sat beside him.

Many of the young people on the stage were friends of hers. Some were people she'd tutored, and others were friends made over the four years she'd lived here in Danbury. Watching them graduate was satisfying, almost as much as hearing Dawn's speech about the road to graduation and the help that Barra had given.

"Barb," Trey whispered in her ear, "you look so proud."

"I am," she answered. While she couldn't be on that stage with so many of her classmates, she'd accomplished a great deal. She had gotten many of them there. She tucked her arm into his, "I'm so proud of my friends."

"They are proud of you," he kissed her cheek. "Proud to call you friend and extended family."

"It's been a long road, and the journey isn't over yet," Mr. O'Hara reminded her.

She nodded; it had been a long road. One that she might not have traveled if Marilla Byrne had her way. She'd had meetings over the last few months with lawyers from the church, she'd signed papers not absolving the church, but recognizing that the church too had been defrauded. While the members of the Gowan family that had been in the church were gone, the damages they had done lived on. But Barra didn't feel it was proper to take it out on the Bishop who had given her freedom.

Dane Ramsey had sold the house in Clark's Town, just as he had said he would. All the furnishings had been put into a warehouse for her to go through. She picked out the things that didn't hold terror or pain. All the bedroom sets had been sold at auction. She couldn't look at them without wanting to hurt someone for the hurt caused her. The money had been put into a trust fund for her, and in investments. Her mother's jewelry had been put into a safety deposit box, for safe keeping. One day, she hoped, she'd be able to look at it, and perhaps wear some of it. For now, it was where no Gowan could touch it.

Her other belongings, taken from her dorm room had been returned. Most of her clothes, she donated to a thrift store, as her grandfather had opened an account for her in several shops. Her laptop had been damaged beyond repair, only the data that she'd saved to external drives and to flash drives still existed. The men from the service that had carted her things off, testified to the fact that it had been Mrs. Byrne and her son who had inflicted the damages to the computer. Her costumes and her props from the game had been returned, undamaged. She knew that Mrs. Byrne had no idea how important those things were, and she was glad to have them back. Mrs. Byrne's son, Robert was still on the run.

She was no longer living at the cottage, as Mr. Morgan died quietly in his sleep in the spring. She didn't feel it looked proper for her to be living at the cottage while Trey was working on the house. Once he moved in, tongues would have wagged. She was staying with her grandfather for the time being, but she wasn't the only grandchild he had staying at the big house. She'd met her cousins, her Aunts and Uncles in the Ramsey Clan, and they had welcomed her with open arms. It took her a bit to get used to them, but she was glad to be among them.

Dane had been true to his word, he'd gotten the albums to her, and had gone so far as to tag the pictures. Faded memories of her parents were coming forward now. She recalled their voices, their faces, and the warm feeling of being with them. Dane had told her they would be so proud of her, of how strong she was. She wondered.

She didn't feel strong, she felt wounded, and scared. She feared she'd carry the abuse and the pain the rest of her life. She wondered if she'd ever trust enough to feel free to marry. Looking at Trey, she knew he'd wait forever if he had to. He was that kind of man. She knew that he wasn't in a rush to get physical. He was self-assured, and gentle, and kind. If there was ever a man she could love, it was Trey. If ever there was anyone who she wanted to be the father of her children, it would be Trey.

She looked back at the stage as Caitlyn held her diploma up. She cheered as loudly as the rest of the O'Hara clan did.

THE BISHOP MET THEM at the cemetery a week after the graduation, Barra, her grandfather, and Trey. The officers with them assured they wouldn't be getting a run-around from the officials in the cemetery office despite the fact that the Bishop had signed off on the exhumation. Marshall Gowan had come to make sure there wasn't any funny business from any member of the Gowan family. He had gotten all the legal papers signed and wasn't about to allow his Mother's memory to mess up his sister's eternity.

"Thank you for this," Barra said. "It goes a long way in your redemption."

"Had I known," he said darkly, "what they had planned..." he shook his head and looked at the Bishop. "We had her buried with all that ceremony, and here she was... a murderess, my sainted mother."

"She's paying for it now on the other side," the Bishop said.

"Too little, too late," He said as they approached the crypt that belonged to the Gowan family. "They lie in there," he pointed. "Mother and Father, my brothers, their wives and between them is a secret that they meant to keep from me. Had my brothers lived, you would have had to deal with them!"

"God is merciful," the Bishop said. "They too paid for their sins. Neither had a child to inherit, and their wives went to the grave with them."

"That's cold," Barra said. "They may have been innocent of any crime."

"Don't believe it," Marshall said. "Your other uncles and aunts on this side of the family were all cut from the same cloth. I'm the black sheep, remember?" The Gowan crypt was covered in carved angels and heavenly symbols. "Gaudy, isn't it?" he groaned.

"They had a skewed view of their importance," the Bishop said.

The cemetery official stood at the door of the crypt. "Everything is ready," he said. "Your funeral director has arranged for pallbearers, and Mrs. Ramsey's remains will be transported to your Cemetery by them." He turned to Barra, "I am so sorry for your loss, and for the pain caused you by the people who took your parent's lives."

"Thank you," she answered. She didn't care at the moment if he were sincere or not.

Trey held her arm, "Breathe," he whispered.

"I am," she responded.

"Just keep breathing."

The door of the crypt was opened, the men from the funeral service that Dane had hired walked in. Moments later, the six men carried the white metal casket out. As it passed Barra she reached out to touch it. When she removed her hand, the men walked down to the hearse.

"Would you care to pay your respects to your grandparents?" the cemetery official asked.

Marshal turned, glaring at the man. "Are you kidding?"

"He doesn't know," she said to her uncle. "Thank you, I don't think that would be proper at this time." He bowed and walked away. "Uncle Marshall," she said softly. "It's not *his* fault."

"I hate this place," he said as they walked away from the crypt. "I have no intentions of being buried with this lot." He assured her. "My parents were hypocrites!"

"Still," Barra said gently, "they were your parents. I am so grateful to you for making this possible."

"I assure you, had I a lick of sense, I'd have checked on the cock and bull story they told me." He looked over at Dane. "I never should have held a grudge against you, I should have known what they told me wasn't kosher."

"You were misinformed," Dane said.

"Once Mary is buried, we can put an end to all of this," Marshall said. "There will be peace."

"The Gowan, Ramsey feud is over," Barra said. "The man who dove the truck is going to prison, and so are the others who took part who are still among the living." Barra didn't mention Robert, but in her heart Barra felt he would be paying for the rest of his life on the run.

"I want to thank you, Mr. Ramsey for allowing me what my parents wouldn't allow you," Marshall said.

Dane smiled softly, "Mary spoke of you often, and I never felt you were my enemy. Roan liked you, who am I to hold a grudge?"

"Yes, but you are allowing me to see my sister put to final rest..." Tears formed in Marshall's eyes. "It touches me."

Barra got into Trey's car and watched as her grandfather got into the car provided by his friend from the funeral home.

"You could have ridden with him," Trey said. "I wouldn't take offense."

"I know that," she said, "but I wanted this time alone with you."

"I'm touched," he teased.

"I've got a feeling my education is at an end," she whispered on a serious note. "The College is not responding to our requests. I may have to apply to another college to finish my courses, and it may take years to get the transripts."

"Is that what you want to do?" he asked.

"I don't know," she said honestly. "When I took the scholarship, I planned on becoming a teacher. Now... I'm not sure."

"Have you given thought to my suggestion?" he asked.

"I have," she nodded. "I think it's too soon to plan a wedding."

"How about an engagement?" Trey suggested, "I do have a ring picked out," he reminded her. "And I'm not giving up."

"It might be a long engagement," she warned.

"Sweetheart, I intend to sweep you off your feet," he retorted. "Danbury is close enough to your grandfather, and your uncle Marshall is willing to come in to see you as often as you'll allow him. Even his wife wants to get to know you."

"I know," she answered, "but I'm still skittish."

"Darling, you're the Raven." He reminded her. "Marshall knows this, he respects you. He'll give you the time, and the space."

"He's still a Gowan..."

Trey took a deep breath, "So were you for most of your life."

"Not really," she said defensively.

"In every way that counted," he argued. "You believed it, you accepted them calling you that and Barbara."

Barra squinted at him, "Smartass," she muttered.

"Yes, my love, I am." He said. "Darling, you have to accept, your father gave you that mark for a reason. He expected you to carry on, to be the Raven for the family Ramsey."

"I'm still not sure what that means," she said. "And if I marry, am I still the Raven?"

Trey snorted, "You will always be the Raven!"

She glared at him, "Trey, that doesn't help."

"You didn't ask for help," he said sassily. "You asked if you will be Raven after we marry, and the answer is yes."

She opened her mouth, then shut it with a snap. He was right of course. She would always be the Raven, just as part of her would always be Barbara Gowan. "You're right."

"I know it," he agreed.

"Are you going to talk to my Grandfather?" she asked.

"Already did," he said smugly.

Barra shook her head, and looked out the window, "What did he say?"

"He suggested we have a long engagement." Trey muttered, then added, "I had to ask what his idea of long was. While it was a bit longer than I thought it should be, he was at least open to the idea of us being engaged."

Barra reached over, "I won't keep you waiting forever," she said. "I promise."

"You're getting used to me," he mused.

"I like that you are with me," she said. "I like that I'm comfortable with you."

"We can build on that," he agreed. "And I have an idea of how to put your history education to work for us at the Orchard. We're going to need a historian as we seek historical landmark status. Who better than someone who has a personal connection? Besides, Old man Morgan left all the legal papers to you."

Barra was quiet the rest of the ride to the cemetery, she had thoughts and emotions she didn't feel the need to share. In the months since she'd left the college, not by choice, she had gone through a federal investigation and trial. She'd seen her great Aunt put behind bars along with the three lawyers who Marshall had turned over to the Federal authorities. She'd changed her name or retaken the legal name of Barra. Often, she still thought of herself as Barbara Gowan. She'd accepted Dane as her grandfather and had come to accept the rest of the Ramsey clan. So many changes, all so fast.

What had seemed to drag out was the battle to regain control of her mother's remains. The Bishop had been most helpful, but even so, there were people who didn't like what she was doing. Some of the Gowan members of the family, second and third cousins, felt she should leave Mary where she was. Mrs. Byrne's son tried to have her barred from entering the cemetery, at the same time he tried to have his mother's conviction overthrown. He failed at both even while he himself was still on the run from the long arm of the law. What power the Gowan's and the Byrne's had was waning.

Barra wasn't surprised that none of the Gowan family, save for Marshall had been there when Mary's remains were removed from the family crypt. 'I'm sorry, Mother,' she thought to herself, 'for any pain my actions cause your soul.'

It was near noon as the hearse pulled through the gated wall of the Saint George and the Dragon cemetery, where for nearly two centuries the Ramsey clan had been laid to rest. Unlike the Gowan's who walled their dead in a gothic crypt, the Ramsey family preferred a garden setting and the sunlight on a hillside in the oldest cemetery in the county. Her grandfather had given her a family history, and he talked about the cemetery. He didn't talk in graven tones, but in gentle reminiscence. She'd been to the cemetery with him, saw where it was her mother would rest. Even though she was missing from the plot, there had been a marker with her name on it.

Barra turned her attention to the road up to the hillside, "Is there a funeral today?" she asked. "There's a lot of cars up there."

"The only hearse is the one with your mom's casket in it." Trey observed. "Barra, isn't that Tim's car?"

She nodded, "And that's Warren's car in front of it." She commented. "What is going on?"

"Don't look at me, I didn't do this." Trey warned.

As they approached, Barra gasped, "Trey, they are dressed in their gaming outfits, with weapons!"

SIGN OF THE RAVEN

"If this is what I think it is, you'd better prepare yourself." He said as he parked behind the limo her grandfather was riding in.

Six young men, three dressed as Anglo lords, and three dressed in the garb of Norse-Celts, stood awaiting the funeral director to exit his car. In solemn modus they took the place of the funeral home's employees. Other members, male warriors and female warriors formed an honor guard with weapons ached for the pallbearers to walk beneath.

Dane turned to Barra, "Was this your idea, sweetheart?" his voice shook with emotions.

"No," she said tearfully. "It was theirs."

"You've got wonderful friends," her grandfather took her arm.

"Yes, yes, I do." She agreed.

Marshal stood behind her, "This would have pleased your mom."

Together they walked through the archway, to the open grave where many chairs were now placed. The Bishop had come to offer support and he and Trey followed Dane and Barra. Behind them were Marshall, his wife and two of his children, the youngest being too young for the ceremony. Mr. and Mrs. O'Hara, and the rest of their family were there also. Mr. and Mrs. Beckett, Warren's parents were also in attendance, as were other people, whose lives Barra had touched. The pallbearers placed the white metal coffin on the stand, and then stood as honor guards.

Dane had asked the Episcopal Bishop to say prayers. He had no idea there would be so many people attending this burial. The Bishop looked at the Catholic Bishop and motioned him to join him.

When everyone who was present had taken their seat, the Bishop spoke. "On behalf of the Ramsey family, let me welcome you, and thank you for coming to give support." He looked at the costumed participants of the honor guard. "Rarely am I privileged to bear witness to the hand of God moving so visibly."

He looked at Dane and Barra seated in the front row with Trey. "I am reminded of the story of the shepherd who searches for the one missing sheep." He smiled at Barra. "How he rejoices when he has found that lost lamb and returns it to his flock. I am also reminded of the story of the good Samaritan," his Eminence said. "Most of all, I want to thank God for making us all his children. The family of humanity, and extended family that knows no race, or religion, but embraces all." He nodded, "That's what I see here today, young people who didn't know the lost lamb in their mist, but who embraced her and made her one of them. And who now join her in returning her mother to her father. Let us not darken our hearts to the ones who caused the pain and suffering. But let us rather pray for their eventual redemption. They are in the hands of God now." He bowed his head, "Let us pray..."

THE CASKET HAD BEEN lowered; dirt had been tossed by the handfuls by each person who attended. Barra stood as the last shovel full was tamped down. "They can't take you away from us now," she said aloud. "You and dad are together again, and no one can split you again."

Trey placed his arm over her shoulders. "You've won," he told her. "Not just the battles, but the war."

"If history has taught me anything," she whispered, for his ears alone, "It's that one should never underestimate one's enemy."

"That's true," he agreed. "But Mrs. Byrne is old and will likely die behind bars. Robert will likely live on the run."

"There are others who would like to pick up her sword," Barra warned. "For that reason, I'm seeking to ensure that none of them can."

Trey looked at her with a raised brow, "What are you planning my Raven?"

"I'm going to fight for my rights to my degrees. I've got two associates that were stolen from me. I want them back, and I'm going to seek restitution from the college as well." She stated. "I've decided I want the degrees to be issued in both names."

"Novel," Trey mused.

"And then I'm going to put in place a scholarship in the names of Roan and Mary Ramsey." She smiled, "That should turn my grandmother in her grave."

"You're a wicked girl," Trey mused.

"You approve," she stated.

"In your own way, you are putting stones on your enemies that cannot be removed. Yes, I approve." Trey nodded. "Your mother was right to demand you be given the mark of the Raven."

"The Raven," Barra said, "is a bird important to both the Celts and the Norse. A bringer of news, a harbinger of ill winds or a foretelling of death."

"The Raven is a bird of great knowledge," Trey countered. "Not just bad things, they warned people of things and were considered a guardian or a protector."

"I want to be that," she said firmly, "I want to protect the ones I hold dear."

"But that's not all you want is it, my love?" he asked in an amused tone. "'There' is something you want more than that."

Barra looked at him, she pursed her lips and nodded. There was more, and there was only one phrase that would encompass the feeling, the overwhelming desire for justice and revenge. "How many of them can we make die?" she glowered.

"That's my girl," he said pulling her close. "Don't ever lose that edge, it will serve you well."

"The battle isn't over," she warned. "They will let us think we won.... But the war has just begun." She leaned into his embrace. "I think this Raven would like a fall wedding."

"Done," he said. "Perhaps a Conquest wedding?" he suggested.

"In the apple orchard," she mused.

"How nice that master's degree certificate is going to look on your office wall, my Raven." He murmured.

She looked up at him, "I will always be the Raven." It was more than a statement; it was a conviction. "I will always fight for what is justice."

"I've a feeling that your mother and father are looking down on you from Heaven and smiling." Trey assured her. "I'm prouder of you than I can say."

"I love you, Trey Lochwood." She whispered what had been on her heart at long last.

He sighed, and pressed his lips to hers.

Fin

Also by Patricia M. Bryce

Book 4 of the Forged Series
The Forged King

Book one of the Forged series
Forged in the Maze

Book two of the Forged Series
Forged Magic

Forged Series book 3
Forged Lives

Standalone
Close to You
The Ghost in the Well
Princess in Hiding
The Brenan Weavers: A Travelers' Novel

Wolfe and Hood
The Guardian of Misty Hollow
Sign of the Raven

Watch for more at patriciambryce.weebly.com.

About the Author

Patricia M. Bryce is a short story author, novelist and cosplayer. She has appeared as Patricia M. Rose in the anthology, Dreams of Steam: Gadgets, edited by Kimberly Richardson and published by Dark Oak Press. When she's not busy writing, she's off being a playtron up at Bristol Renaissance Faire. You can learn more at https://www.facebook.com/PaisleyRose1

Read more at patriciambryce.weebly.com.

Printed in the USA
CPSIA information can be obtained
at www.ICGtesting.com
LVHW042314021023
759959LV00005B/68